What's happened to Todd?

Tim Davis passed the ball to Todd Wilkins just before one of the Big Mesa players tried to steal it. There were three seconds left. Todd was open for the final shot.

A Big Mesa player came charging at him, trying to stop him. Todd took aim. The crowd rose to their feet. Someone started chanting, "Wil-kins, Wil-kins, Wil-kins," and soon all the Gladiator fans picked up the chant. Todd was soaked with sweat.

Two seconds left. He measured the distance from the basket, aimed, and shot.

The ball hit the backboard. It hovered on the rim. Go in, go in, Todd prayed. The ball circled and circled the rim. The gym was silent, as if the whole crowd was holding their breath.

Finally the ball tipped to the outside of the rim and fell to the ground.

There were cheers on the Big Mesa side of the gym, groans on the Sweet Valley side. The buzzer sounded, signaling the end of the game. The Gladiators had lost their first game of the season.

And it was all Todd's fault.

Bantam Books in the SWEET VALLEY TWINS AND FRIENDS series.
Ask your bookseller for the books you have missed.

SWEET VALLEY TWINS
AND FRIENDS

Todd Runs Away

Written by
Jamie Suzanne

Created by
FRANCINE PASCAL

BANTAM BOOKS
NEW YORK · TORONTO · LONDON · SYDNEY · AUCKLAND

RL 4, 008-012

TODD RUNS AWAY

A Bantam Book / March 1994

*Sweet Valley High® and Sweet Valley Twins and Friends® are
registered trademarks of Francine Pascal*

Conceived by Francine Pascal

*Produced by Daniel Weiss Associates, Inc.
33 West 17th Street
New York, NY 10011*

Cover art by James Mathewuse

ISBN: 0-553-48100-2

Published simultaneously in the United States and Canada

*Bantam Books are published by Bantam Books, a division of Bantam
Doubleday Dell Publishing Group, Inc. Its trademark, consisting of the
words "Bantam Books" and the portrayal of a rooster, is Registered in
U.S. Patent and Trademark Office and in other countries. Marca
Registrada. Bantam Books, 1540 Broadway, New York, New York 10036.*

PRINTED IN THE UNITED STATES OF AMERICA

OPM   0 9 8 7 6 5 4 3 2 1

One

"Yo, Wilkins!" Rick Hunter shouted across the locker room. "Awesome game!"

It was late Friday afternoon, and the Sweet Valley Middle School boys' basketball team, the Gladiators, had just won their fifth straight game of the season.

"Thanks, Rick!" Todd Wilkins yelled back. "You had a great game too."

"Not as good as yours," Rick said, giving him the thumbs-up.

Todd grinned. All the guys on the team had played well, but Todd had made the winning shot.

Tim Davis looked up as Todd sat on the bench next to him. "You were pretty impressive out there today, Wilkins," he said as he unlaced his new pump basketball shoes.

"Thanks, buddy," Todd said casually, as if he were used to being congratulated all the time by the team's star player. But he could hardly keep from grinning with pride as he opened his locker. Todd was the only sixth-grader on the varsity team, and having someone like Tim tell him he was a good player was a pretty big deal.

Just then Bruce Patman, a seventh-grade player, strolled into the locker room and sat down on the other side of Tim. "Yeah, you did all right, Wilkins," Bruce said as he opened his locker and began fixing his hair in the mirror he'd hung inside the door. "But you wouldn't have made that last shot if it wasn't for my assist."

Tim rolled his eyes. "What about the three times Todd assisted *you*?" he asked Bruce.

Bruce shrugged. "It's a team sport."

Tim nodded. "Exactly."

Todd finished tying his sneakers. He knew better than to pay too much attention to Bruce. Just because the Patmans owned half of Sweet Valley, Bruce thought that made him king of the school. "Well," Todd said as he finished dressing, "I guess I'll see you guys at practice on Tuesday."

"Later," Rick said.

Todd started for the door.

"Hey, Wilkins!" Peter Jeffries called after him. "You forgot something."

Todd turned around. His knee braces were lying folded up on the bench where he'd left them.

"Thanks," he said, going back to toss them into his locker. The braces were kind of a pain, in Todd's opinion. He wore them only to make his father happy. Mr. Wilkins had been a basketball superstar on his own high school team, and he always told Todd that the only thing that had kept him from a career in professional basketball was a bad knee injury. For that reason he always insisted that Todd be extra careful about protecting his knees.

Todd walked out of the locker room into the lobby of the gym, where he was nearly crushed by the crowd of friends and fans waiting to congratulate him.

Todd's friend Ken Matthews slapped him on the back. "Way to go, Todd," he said. "You were great out there."

"Thanks, Ken," Todd said. "But I didn't win by myself. We've got a really good team."

"Yeah, well, the rest of the really good team was lucky to have you out there today," Winston Egbert put in. "You were hot!"

"Thanks, Win." Todd grinned. Winston was the only male member of the Boosters, the middle school's cheering squad. "The Boosters deserve some credit too. You guys had the crowd worked up before we even got out on the court."

"Speaking of Boosters," Ken commented, "it looks like the Boosters' chapter of the Todd Wilkins Fan Club is headed this way."

"Make that the *Unicorn* chapter," Winston said, making a face.

Todd turned to see Jessica Wakefield, Lila Fowler, Ellen Riteman, and Janet Howell pushing their way through the crowd toward them. All four girls were members of the Unicorn Club, an exclusive group of the prettiest and most popular girls in school. The Unicorns had started the Boosters, and Winston had had to work hard to convince them to let him join. He and Amy Sutton were still the only non-Unicorn members of the Boosters.

"That was one of the most exciting games I ever cheered for," Janet said, giving Todd a big smile.

"Me too," Jessica agreed, tossing back her long blond hair. "Totally awesome."

"Totally, *totally* awesome," Ellen corrected her. She turned to Todd. "We were even talking about making you an honorary Unicorn!"

Todd grinned. "I don't know about that, Ellen. Purple's not really my color." Purple—the color of royalty—was the official color of the Unicorn Club. Every member tried to wear something purple every day.

"He's right," Janet said, looking Todd up and down critically. "He looks better in blue. You know, Todd, you're really lucky the team uniforms happen to be blue. If they were yellow, you'd be in real trouble."

Ellen shrugged. "I still think they should change the official school color to purple."

"Oh, please, Ellen," Lila snapped impatiently. "How many times do we have to discuss this?"

"Really, Ellen," Jessica agreed. "After all, if every loser on every middle school sports team wore purple all the time, it wouldn't be as special." She gave Todd a dazzling smile. "Not that any of the basketball players are losers, of course."

Ellen pouted. "I still think purple uniforms would be cool."

As the four girls continued to argue, Todd looked around for Jessica's twin sister, Elizabeth. He was glad that their friendship was back to normal again. Around Valentine's Day the month before, he and Ken had played a few jokes on Elizabeth and Amy Sutton, and things had gotten a little out of hand. For a while it had looked as though Elizabeth would never forgive him. But after she had made him sing "Feelings" onstage in front of everyone at the Valentine's Day dance, they had declared a truce. Finally he saw her standing on the other side of the lobby. "Elizabeth!" he called, waving. He took a few steps away from the arguing Unicorns, who didn't even notice him leaving. Winston and Ken had already wandered away into the crowd.

Elizabeth smiled and waved back. "Hi, Todd!" she called out. "Great game!"

But as Todd started to fight his way through the crowd toward her, he found his father suddenly blocking his way, a proud smile on his face.

"Great game, son!" Mr. Wilkins said, slapping Todd on the back. "I was just talking to Coach Cassels about how far you've come. You're even better than I was at your age. I'm proud of you."

Todd smiled at his father. Mr. Wilkins had been coaching Todd ever since he could remember. He tried to come to as many of Todd's games as his busy work schedule permitted. "I'm glad you could make it," Todd said. "I thought you had a meeting at work."

His father winked. "I rescheduled it. I had a feeling you were going to have a great game, and I didn't want to miss it."

"Well, I'm glad your feeling was right."

"Of course it was," Mr. Wilkins said. "I wouldn't expect anything less from you, son—you're a superstar already, and you're only going to get better. Now, how about we go out to dinner and celebrate, just the two of us?"

"Sounds great, Dad." Todd glanced across the lobby and saw that Elizabeth was still waiting patiently for him. "Just hold on a second while I say good-bye to Elizabeth, OK?"

"No problem," his father replied. "I'll wait right here."

Todd hurried over to Elizabeth. She smiled at him. "Congratulations, Todd," she said. "You were great."

Todd grinned. As many times as he'd heard those words today, hearing them from Elizabeth was somehow better than hearing them from anybody else. "Thanks," he said. "I was pretty nervous out there. The team really wants to keep this winning streak going. We only have to win two more games to qualify for the district championship tournament."

"I can imagine how nervous you would be," Elizabeth replied. "But it looked like you were having fun, too."

"I was," Todd admitted. One of the things he liked most about Elizabeth was that she almost always seemed to know just what he was thinking or how he was feeling. And she didn't get all mushy over him, the way some girls got over guys.

"Hey, you two," Jessica said, rushing over. "A bunch of us are going to celebrate at the Dairi Burger. Want to come?"

"Sure, that sounds like fun," Elizabeth said.

Seeing the twins standing next to each other, Todd found himself noticing again how different Elizabeth and Jessica were from each other. The twins looked so much alike—from their long, golden-blond hair to their sparkling blue-green eyes—that strangers often had trouble telling them apart. But people who knew them knew just how different they were in almost every way *except* looks. Elizabeth was the more serious and sensitive twin. She enjoyed school, especially English class, and loved working on the *Sweet Valley Sixers*, the class newspaper she had helped start.

Jessica, on the other hand, never spent any more time than she absolutely had to on schoolwork. She preferred to hang out with the other members of the Unicorn Club and gossip about boys, rock stars, and clothes.

Todd glanced over at his waiting father. "I can't," he said. "I'm going out to dinner with my dad."

"Oh, that's nice," Elizabeth said, but Todd thought she looked a little disappointed. "How about if you and I go for a sundae at Casey's tomorrow afternoon, Elizabeth?" he suggested.

Elizabeth smiled. "I'd love to," she said. "I'll see you tomorrow."

"See you," Todd said happily, and he ran back to his father.

"I was talking to Coach Cassels after the game. You know, he considers you one of the best players on the team," Mr. Wilkins told Todd as they walked across the school parking lot toward their car. "He says it's because you're such a hard worker, and that whenever you're on the court you always make basketball your top priority." His father patted him on the back. "That's how you get to be the best."

Todd smiled. "I guess I played a pretty good game today," he admitted. "But I still have a lot to learn. My foul shooting is a little off."

His father shrugged. "You never stop learning, no matter how good you get. But I think I can give you a few pointers. How about if we shoot some baskets this weekend?"

"That sounds great," Todd said.

His father nodded thoughtfully. "Foul shots were always my weak point too. They're not as easy as they look. One thing my coach told me is to shoot for the back of the rim."

"I'll try it," Todd said, climbing into the car. "But I have to admit, right now my top priority is to inhale about three pizzas and a cheeseburger. And that's just for starters. I'm *starving*."

His father laughed. "Hey, for a basketball star like you," he said, "you can have whatever you want."

"So who's going to write the story on the basketball game for the *Sixers* this week?" Elizabeth asked Amy at the Dairi Burger a little while later. The two of them had taken a quiet booth in the back of the restaurant, as far away as possible from where the Unicorns were noisily flirting with the members of the basketball team.

Amy raised her eyebrows and smiled wryly. "Maybe I'd better write it," she said. "*I* don't have a boyfriend on the team."

Elizabeth grinned. "Are you saying you don't think I'd be objective?" she asked, acting insulted.

Amy raised her hands in surrender. "Oh, no," she said. "Not at all. Just because Todd happens to be the star of the team . . ." She ducked as Elizabeth pretended to flick a spoonful of whipped cream at her.

"Actually," Elizabeth said when they stopped laughing, "I was going to ask if you *would* write the basketball article this time. I was thinking of doing a story about the new creative-writing class that's starting."

Amy nodded. "That sounds like it's going to be a lot of fun, doesn't it?"

"Definitely," Elizabeth said. She already knew she wanted to be a professional writer when she grew up. She had often dreamed of becoming a prize-winning journalist for a major newspaper. But she sometimes wondered what it would be like to write short stories or novels, like her favorite mystery writer, Amanda Howard. She figured the creative-writing course that her English teacher, Mr. Bowman, had announced the week before would be a perfect way to find out. The class would be limited to a dozen students, and Mr. Bowman was going to announce who had been chosen for it on Monday. "I just hope I get in."

Amy rolled her eyes. "You'll get in if anyone does, Elizabeth. You're the best writer in our class."

Before Elizabeth could answer, there was an outburst of laughter from the Unicorn table on the other side of the room. Elizabeth glanced over to the booth where Jessica and her friends were sitting. Jessica had her hands raised, describing something. Suddenly her face reddened, and she lowered her arms quickly and crossed them over her chest.

Elizabeth's eyes widened. She recognized the motion—she had found herself doing the exact same thing a lot lately, especially when she was wearing a tight shirt. She was realizing that it might be time to start wearing a bra. Could Jessica be thinking the same thing?

"What are you staring at?" Amy asked, following Elizabeth's gaze.

Elizabeth shook herself. "Oh, nothing," she said. Even though Amy was her best friend after Jessica, Elizabeth didn't really feel comfortable bringing up the subject of bras with her—especially since Amy showed no signs of needing to wear one anytime soon. "What were you saying about the writing class?" she asked to change the subject.

"I was saying that you'll definitely get in," Amy repeated patiently. "I just hope I do too. I wonder what the new teacher will be like."

Elizabeth shrugged. "I don't know. But I overheard Mr. Bowman telling Mr. Clark that it was someone just out of graduate school."

There was another burst of laughter from the Unicorns' booth. Elizabeth glanced over and saw that Jessica still had her arms crossed over her chest. Elizabeth took a deep breath. As soon as she got the chance, she was going to have to talk to Jessica about getting bras.

"Now, Ms. Wakefield," Amy said, pulling a

pad and pen from her purse, "what did you, as an *objective* observer, think of today's basketball game?"

Elizabeth looked back at Amy and grinned. "Objectively," she said, "I think the Gladiators are awesome."

Two

◇

It was late Saturday morning. Jessica was in the kitchen pouring herself a glass of juice when her fourteen-year-old brother, Steven, walked into the kitchen and sat down at the table.

"That T-shirt's a little lumpy, don't you think, Jessica?" Steven said, glancing at Jessica's chest. "Maybe you should iron it."

She gave him a withering stare. "I have no idea what you're talking about," she said icily, crossing her arms over her chest. Besides being the biggest eater in the world, Steven could sometimes be the biggest jerk. She couldn't believe he was making jokes about her chest. Only recently she had started noticing that she'd grown a little there, and she hadn't thought it was that obvious yet. "You're about as funny as the warts on your feet, Steven," she said.

Steven guffawed. "Speaking of warts . . ." he said.

Jessica tossed her hair over her shoulders. "Oh, shut up!" she snapped, wondering how many years they'd give her in prison for strangling her brother. She grabbed a couple of apples from the fruit bin and took aim at his head. "Speaking of warts, there's a huge one growing between your shoulders."

At that moment Mrs. Wakefield walked into the kitchen. "What are you doing?" she demanded, taking the apples from Jessica's hand.

Jessica pasted on her most innocent smile. "I was just giving Steven a snack."

Mrs. Wakefield looked skeptical. "I think Steven's old enough to get his own snacks."

"Whatever you say, Mom," Jessica said.

Steven began to snicker. "Warts," he whispered as she walked past.

Jessica ground her teeth and did her best to ignore him. When she reached her bedroom, she closed the door behind her and stood in front of the full-length mirror, looking at herself sideways. Most of the seventh- and eighth-grade Unicorns had been wearing bras for ages, and Ellen had bought her first one a couple of months ago. Maybe Jessica needed one now too.

She plopped down on her bed. She wondered if Elizabeth was noticing the same thing. *She must be*, she thought. After all, they looked so much alike in every other way—why would this be any different?

Still, Jessica remembered that they hadn't gotten their periods at the exact same time. Elizabeth had gotten hers first. Jessica remembered how humiliated she had felt at being left behind. She sighed. She didn't want to make Elizabeth feel as bad now as she had felt then. Pushing herself off the bed, she began to pace the room.

As she walked toward her night table, she noticed the new issue of *SMASH!* on top of her other magazines. Her mother must have put it up in her room that morning after the mail came. She sat down on the edge of her bed and began to flip through the pages. Suddenly her eye fell on an ad—for Dreamline bras.

Her eyes widened. "I've got it!" she exclaimed aloud.

She tore the ad from the magazine, then hurried through the bathroom that connected the twins' bedrooms and knocked on Elizabeth's door. There was no answer. Easing open the door, she peeked inside. All clear.

She ran to Elizabeth's closet and hid the ad under a pair of sneakers. Elizabeth would definitely see it there. Then she bolted back to her room and closed the door.

She grinned at her reflection in the mirror. "The perfect way to break the ice," she whispered.

"I'll stop by your house and pick you up in half an hour, OK?"

"Great," Elizabeth said. She hung up the phone in the living room and headed to her bedroom to change. She was looking forward to her date with Todd, but she was also still distracted by her thoughts of the day before. She wanted to find out if Jessica was thinking about needing a bra too, but she didn't quite know how to ask her.

Elizabeth wouldn't trade her own group of friends for Jessica's in a million years, but she couldn't help thinking that hanging around with the Unicorns might actually have its advantages at times. She figured they probably talked about things like bras all the time—after all, Elizabeth had heard them discuss practically every other article of clothing in excruciating detail. Jessica probably already knew everything there was to know about bras.

Elizabeth sighed. Normally she could talk with her twin about anything, but this was something new and strange for her. The truth was, it was sort of . . . embarrassing. Still, she had to face it sometime. *And there's no time like the present*, she thought, taking a deep breath.

She knocked on Jessica's bedroom door. There was no answer, so she carefully opened the door. "Jess?" she said. She could hear the shower running in the bathroom they shared.

She quietly closed the door and stood indecisively in the hallway for a moment, biting her lip. Another thought had just occurred to her. She had gotten her period before Jessica had, and Jessica had been pretty upset about it. What if it was the same thing with getting a bra? After all, Elizabeth *was* the older twin by four minutes. She could have been mistaken about what she thought she'd seen at the Dairi Burger.

She sighed again, wishing there was some way to find out for sure if Jessica needed a bra, without coming right out and asking her. Maybe she could think of a way to bring up the general subject of bras and see how Jessica reacted. Then she could decide how to go from there.

After her date she would think about it some more, she decided. At the moment she had to hurry up and change before Todd arrived. In her bedroom, she searched her closet for something to wear. Her new pale-blue sweater and her black jeans seemed like the way to go. But when she put the sweater on, she nearly gagged. "I look like I have *mosquito bites* on my chest!" she told her reflection. She pulled at the front of the sweater, trying to loosen it, but it didn't help. She would have to wear something else.

She finally decided on an old, bulky green sweater. It wasn't what she ordinarily would have chosen for a date, and it was a little hot for a sunny day like today, but at least it hid her chest.

After quickly running a brush through her hair and pulling it back into a ponytail, she went to the closet for her sneakers. As she picked them up she saw that a piece of paper had been hidden under them. It was a page torn out of a magazine—an ad for Dreamline bras. She picked it up. *Now, how did that get here?* she wondered. But then her eyes lit up. Dreamline bras! That gave her a great idea!

She tiptoed to the bathroom door. The shower was still running. Usually it annoyed her that Jessica took such long showers, but right now she was glad.

She ran to Jessica's bedroom, bra ad in hand. But just as she closed Jessica's door behind her, the shower stopped. "Oh, no!" she gasped.

She hurriedly scanned the room for someplace to hide the ad where Jessica would be sure to find it. Her eyes settled on the latest issue of *SMASH!*, Jessica's favorite magazine. She quickly stuck the ad underneath the magazine, then tiptoed out of the bedroom. As soon as she'd closed Jessica's door she heard the bathroom door inside Jessica's room open. "Whew, that was a close one!" she muttered.

"Elizabeth! Todd's here!" It was her mother calling her from downstairs.

"I'll be right there," she said, feeling relieved. *What a perfect way to break the ice,* she thought.

"I'll have two scoops of chocolate peanut-butter cup with hot fudge," Elizabeth said to the waitress at Casey's Place a while later.

"I'll have a Casey's Special," Todd said.

"You must be hungry," Elizabeth teased, raising her eyebrows and glancing at the picture on the menu of four scoops of ice cream on top of a chocolate brownie, smothered in chocolate sauce.

Todd shrugged and grinned. "Hey, what can I say? Basketball burns up a lot of energy," he said. He handed the waitress his menu.

Just then Tim Davis walked into the restaurant with Jim Sturbridge and Belinda Layton. Belinda was a Unicorn, but she was also very athletic. Elizabeth didn't really know her that well, but she knew that she and Jim had been a couple for a few months now. She also knew that Jim and Tim were neighbors and that they liked to play basketball together. Jim was a sixth-grader and hadn't made the team this year, but Elizabeth was sure he'd make it next year.

"Hi, Todd," Tim said. "Hi, Elizabeth." He slid into the booth next to Todd. Jim sat down beside Elizabeth, but Belinda remained standing.

"Hi, guys," Todd said. "What's up?"

"Oh, we just came in to get a snack. The three of us were thinking about shooting some hoops over at the high school later. What do you say?"

Todd shrugged. "Sorry, " he said, "but I already made plans to practice with my dad. He wants to give me a few pointers."

Tim rolled his eyes. "You poor guy! My dad's always trying to give me pointers too. He's a great dad, but he's not exactly Michael Jordan, if you know what I mean."

"*I* know what you mean," Jim said. "I have the same problem."

Todd smiled. "Not me," he said. "My dad probably would've made it to the pros if he hadn't wrecked his knees."

Jim's eyes widened. "Really?" he asked, sounding impressed.

Todd nodded. "Yeah. He was a really good player. That's why I have to wear those knee braces. He doesn't want me to ruin my knees like he ruined his."

The waitress brought over Todd's and Elizabeth's ice cream. "Can I get you a menu?" she asked Tim, Jim, and Belinda.

"Sure," Tim said.

Elizabeth felt a twinge of annoyance. Were they going to sit there and *eat* with them? So much for their date!

"But why don't you can bring the menus over there," Belinda told the waitress, pointing to a booth on the other side of the room. She smiled at Elizabeth. "I think this booth is a little too small for all of us."

Elizabeth gave Belinda a little smile of thanks.

"Whatever. As long as I get some ice cream, I don't care where we sit," Tim said, eyeing Todd's Casey's Special. "Hey, that looks great."

Todd shielded his ice cream with his hands. "Teamwork's teamwork," he said. "But when it comes to a Casey's Special, I draw the line."

Everyone laughed, and Tim, Belinda, and Jim headed toward their own booth.

"So what do you think of the new creative-writing class?" Elizabeth asked Todd as soon as the others were gone. She had started working on her *Sixers* article about the class that morning.

Todd shrugged. "It sounds all right," he said, digging into his ice cream. "I mean, it's not really my thing. But it sounds like something you'd like."

Elizabeth swallowed a spoonful of ice cream. "I'd love it!" she said. "I like writing for the *Sixers*, but newspaper articles and fictional stories are two different things. I'd love to write a book someday."

"A book?" said Todd. "Not me. It would take forever!" He looked up from his bowl, an alarmed look on his face. "Hey, how much writing do you think will be required for this course, anyway? I mean, if by some miracle I did get chosen, I wouldn't want to have to spend all my free time writing novels and stuff." Elizabeth laughed. "I doubt the teacher will expect us to write novels. It's just a six-week course."

"Good," Todd mumbled, leaning over his bowl again and scooping up some ice cream. "Still, writing any kind of story at all sounds like a lot of work. Especially for kids who play sports or do other activities."

"I guess it might take up more time than most classes. But I think it'll be worth it," Elizabeth said. "Anyway, on Monday Mr. Bowman's posting the list of students who'll be in the class. Maybe we'll both get chosen. That would be fun, wouldn't it?"

Todd swallowed a huge mouthful of brownie and ice cream. "I don't know," he mumbled.

Elizabeth looked surprised.

"I mean, I just don't know if I'd like it that much. I mean, it would be fun being with *you*, but I'm not really interested in writing. Anyway, like I said, I seriously doubt I'll get in. I don't know how to write."

"But that's the whole point," Elizabeth said, shaking her spoon at him. "If you already knew how to write, you wouldn't have to learn."

Todd laughed. "I guess not," he said. "But I don't think I can do it anyway. It meets on Tuesdays and Thursdays, the same as basketball practice."

"You could still make it to practice on time," Elizabeth pointed out.

"Well," Todd said, "I guess it all boils down to who Mr. Bowman picks, right? And he probably won't choose me."

"You never know," Elizabeth said with a shrug.

Three

On Monday morning, as Elizabeth was getting ready for school, there was a loud knock at her door. "Who is it?" she asked.

"It's me," Jessica said.

"Come on in," Elizabeth called, frowning. Since when had her twin ever bothered to knock? Usually she just barged in whenever she felt like it.

Jessica walked into the room, looking worried.

"What's wrong?" Elizabeth asked.

Jessica let out a dramatic sigh and flopped down on Elizabeth's bed. "I can't find my new purple high-tops *anywhere*. You know, the ones with the striped laces?" She sighed again, louder. "There's a Unicorn meeting today, and I really wanted to wear them."

Elizabeth shrugged. "Do you remember where you saw them last?"

"I'm not exactly sure. I thought they might be in here." Jessica sat up and looked around the room hopefully.

"Well, you're out of luck, Jess," Elizabeth said, walking over to her dresser and picking up her hairbrush. "I just cleaned my room, and I didn't see them."

Jessica's face fell for a moment. Then she brightened. "Oh, I just remembered. I think I left them by the kitchen door yesterday. Mom probably thought they were yours and put them in here without you noticing."

Elizabeth shook her head and gazed at her sister's reflection in the mirror. "Jess, why would Mom think *I* would wear *purple* sneakers?"

"Oh, I don't know, Lizzie," Jessica said impatiently. "But I've searched the whole rest of the house already. Can't I just look around in here for them? I just have this bizarre feeling they're in your room somewhere."

"Fine. Whatever," Elizabeth said, looking at her twin in puzzlement. She didn't know what Jessica was up to, but she didn't have time to think about it right now. She was running a little late since it had taken her longer than usual to find something to wear. More and more of her shirts had started to look strange without a bra underneath them. She had finally settled on a baggy navy-blue T-shirt that Steven had recently outgrown. "Just try not to mess everything up too much," she told Jessica.

"Thanks," Jessica said. She rushed to the closet and tossed Elizabeth's sneakers aside with a triumphant expression. Then her face fell. "Where is it?" she said.

"Where's what?" Elizabeth asked.

Jessica looked as though she'd just gotten caught cheating on a test. "Um, my shoes," she said. "Where are my shoes?"

Elizabeth shook her head. Jessica could be very strange sometimes.

Jessica began tossing all of Elizabeth's shoes out of the closet.

"Stop it!" Elizabeth said, annoyed. "You're making a mess!"

"But I have to find it—I mean, *them*," Jessica said.

"Well, let me help," Elizabeth offered. "It's possible to look for things without tearing the place apart."

She joined Jessica at the closet. Carefully and methodically, she began checking each pair of shoes in the closet. "They're not here," she said finally.

"They've got to be!"

Elizabeth frowned. "Why?" she asked. "They're probably in your room, buried under something."

"No, I'm positive they're in here," Jessica said stubbornly.

But Elizabeth's own words had just reminded her about the ad for Dreamline bras she'd hidden under the magazine in Jessica's room. This was the perfect opportunity to pretend to stumble upon the ad. "Hey, Jess," she said, pulling Jessica away from the closet. "Why don't I help you search *your* room?"

Jessica shook her head. "No, they're not there. I checked."

Elizabeth dragged her toward the door. "Let's check again," she said. "Maybe you didn't look carefully enough."

"But . . ." Jessica said, gazing forlornly over her shoulder at Elizabeth's closet.

"Come on!" Elizabeth said, finally managing to pull Jessica out of the room.

In Jessica's room, Elizabeth briefly pretended to search under the bed and beneath some of the clothes heaped on Jessica's chair and desk. Then she headed over to Jessica's nightstand and the pile of magazines.

"My shoes wouldn't be inside a *magazine*," Jessica said irritably.

Elizabeth gulped. "Yeah, I know. I, um, I noticed you had the latest issue of *Smash!*. I just wanted to see it."

"Since when do you read *Smash!*?" Jessica demanded. "You're always telling me how stupid and trendy it is."

"Well, uh, I . . ." Elizabeth stammered, thinking fast. "I saw that Johnny Buck is on the cover this month. He looks pretty cute, doesn't he?" She grabbed the magazine, making sure to knock the

Dreamline ad off the table at the same time. "Oh, look, Jess!" she said, trying to sound surprised. "What's that?"

"What's what?" Jessica demanded. "And by the way, since when do *you* think Johnny Bu—"

"This ad," Elizabeth said quickly, shoving it under Jessica's nose.

Jessica gasped and grabbed the ad out of her hands. "The Dreamline bras ad! But this is supposed to be in your clos—I mean . . ."

Elizabeth's eyes widened. So *that's* how the ad had gotten in her closet! "*You* put the ad in my closet?" she asked incredulously. "But I put it in here so *you'd* find it!"

The twins stared at each other for a moment. "Why did you want me to find it?" Jessica asked finally.

Elizabeth glanced at the ad, and then at Jessica. "You put it in *my* closet first," she pointed out. "You tell me."

Jessica bit her lip. Then she glanced at Elizabeth's shirt. "Isn't that shirt a little big for you?" she commented.

Elizabeth glanced at the loose jacket Jessica was wearing. "You seem to be into baggy stuff yourself these days, Jess."

Their eyes met and they started laughing.

"We need bras!" they said in unison, collapsing on Jessica's bed with laughter.

"I can't believe you went to all that trouble to

find out if I thought I needed a bra!" Elizabeth said at last.

"What about *you*?" Jessica replied. "You put it back in here!"

"Have you talked to Mom about this yet?" Elizabeth asked when they'd finally gotten themselves under control.

Jessica shook her head, looking embarrassed. "I wasn't quite sure how to bring it up to her," she admitted. "Anyway, I wanted to talk to you about it first."

"Me too," Elizabeth said. "Besides, Mom's been so busy with that hotel project that I didn't really want to bother her right now." Mrs. Wakefield was an interior designer, and her latest project involved redecorating several floors of a luxury hotel.

"That's true," Jessica said. "Let's just pick some up for ourselves. We can tell Mom about it when her project is finished and she's back to normal."

Elizabeth glanced at the ad. "This ad says they sell Dreamline bras at Kendall's."

"Hmm," Jessica said. "Sounds good. Janet and Kimberly are always talking about how comfortable Dreamline bras are." She gazed at the ad thoughtfully. "I think we should each get one, Lizzie," she said. "Then we can get Mom to take us back later if we think we need some more. I wonder if they have them in purple."

"I guess this means we should plan a trip to Kendall's, then," Elizabeth said, hiding a smile.

She had been right about the Unicorns' bra discussions! It was kind of a relief that she and Jessica would be going to buy the bras themselves instead of asking their mother to take them. Normally Elizabeth felt she could talk about almost anything with her mother, but for some reason this was different. She wasn't sure she was ready for anyone— even her mother—to know just how much she was growing up.

Luckily, she had Jessica to share this with. Since they'd started middle school the twins hadn't really done as many things together as they'd used to. This would be a chance for them to share something special and important.

"But when can we go buy them?" Jessica asked, interrupting Elizabeth's thoughts. "Kendall's is usually so crowded, and I don't want anyone to see us. It's too embarrassing."

Elizabeth nodded. "How about Wednesday after school?"

"There's a pep rally on Wednesday," Jessica reminded her.

Elizabeth raised her eyebrows. "Exactly," she said. "Everyone will be at the pep rally, so we definitely won't run into anyone at Kendall's."

Jessica grinned. "You're brilliant, Lizzie!"

"Have you seen the new teacher yet?" Amy asked Pamela Jacobson and Elizabeth at school later on Monday. The three girls were standing in front of the bulletin board. The names of the students who would be in the creative-writing class were listed on a piece of yellow paper tacked to the bulletin board. All three of them were on the list, along with Maria Slater, Nora Mercandy, Sophia Rizzo, Patrick Morris, Randy Mason, Mandy Miller, Julie Porter, Cammi Adams—and, Elizabeth was happy to see, Todd Wilkins.

"Nope. But Maria said she saw a really cute young guy talking to Mr. Clark before school this morning," Pamela said. "She said Mr. Clark gave him a key to one of the offices."

"That must be the new teacher!" Elizabeth said excitedly. "I'm so glad we all got into this class— it's going to be great!"

"What's going to be great?" Maria asked as she came around the corner. Her dark hair was pushed back with a gold headband that offset her smooth mocha-colored skin.

"Hi, Maria," Elizabeth said, gesturing for her to join them. "The creative-writing class. Pamela says you saw the new teacher."

Maria laughed. "I said I thought he *might* be the new teacher," she said. "I'm not positive."

"Who else would be getting an office key?" Pamela asked.

Maria shrugged. "Anyway, I'm psyched too. When I heard it was limited to twelve students I didn't think I had a chance."

Elizabeth giggled. "You sound like Todd. He

kept saying he wouldn't get picked. I can't wait to see his face when he finds out!"

"Finds out what?"

Elizabeth turned around. Todd was standing right behind her. "You made it into the writing class!" she told him happily.

Todd hurried over to the bulletin board and looked at the list. "Oh, no," he muttered, shaking his head.

"What's the matter?" Maria said, glancing at the other girls in confusion. "The course is going to be fun."

Todd ran a hand through his dark hair. "How am I going to have time to take the class and still make it to basketball practice?"

Elizabeth looked helplessly at the other girls, then at Todd. "The class is over at three thirty, and you don't start practice until quarter to four. You'll have plenty of time to make it."

"What about all the extra work?" he said.

Amy shrugged. "It's too late. You're on the list."

"Not for long," Todd argued. "I'm going to tell Mr. Bowman to take me *off* the list." He started toward Mr. Bowman's office.

"But you can't, Todd," Elizabeth called after him.

Todd turned around. "Why can't I?"

Elizabeth was a little taken aback at the tone of Todd's voice. "Because," she said, "Mr. Bowman had an appointment and won't be in until this afternoon. I went to talk to him about an article for the *Sixers*, and Mr. Davis was filling in for him."

"Great," Todd said under his breath.

Elizabeth looked from Maria to Amy to Pamela, and then back at Todd. "Maybe you should just give the class a try," she said. "You may like it—you never know."

"I *do* know," Todd said. "And I'm not going to like it, because I'm not going to be in it." He turned and stormed off to class.

"Hey, Todd. You want to go to the Dairi Burger?" Aaron asked. The final bell had just rung, and a bunch of students were heading over to the popular restaurant for an afternoon snack.

"I can't," Todd said. "There's something important I have to do."

"What's more important than your stomach?" Ken asked.

Todd sighed. "Mr. Bowman put me in that new creative-writing class. It meets the same days as my basketball practice. I'm going to tell him I can't do it."

Patrick shrugged. "I don't know if that will work. I heard it wasn't optional. Anyway, I'm in the class too, and it sounds like it might be cool."

Todd shook his head. "Maybe, but I'm still going to get out of it. Basketball is my first priority, and that's that."

Mr. Bowman was grading some papers when Todd walked into his classroom. "Uh, hi, Mr.

Bowman. Can I talk to you for a minute?" Todd asked.

Mr. Bowman put down his pen and straightened his tie, which was blue with red polka dots on it. It clashed with his olive-green suit, and Todd tried not to wince. Mr. Bowman was well-known around Sweet Valley Middle School for his terrible taste in clothes.

"Sit down, Todd," Mr. Bowman said, gesturing to a chair beside his desk. He smiled. "Congratulations on making the cut for the new writing class," he added.

Todd cleared his throat. "Actually, Mr. Bowman, that's why I'm here."

"Oh?"

"Yes, sir. The fact is, I'm not interested in creative writing, and I'd like you to take me off the list."

Mr. Bowman leaned back in his chair. "I see," he said. "Have you ever written a story?"

Todd shrugged. "No, not really."

"Well, how do you know you're not interested, then?"

"I just do," Todd said.

Mr. Bowman nodded thoughtfully. "I'm sorry, Todd, but I'm afraid it's impossible for me to take you off the list. I've already made my decision."

"But, Mr. Bowman—"

"Listen, Todd. The reason I chose you was that you seem to have a flair for writing. I've noticed it in the book reports you've written for my class."

"But writing book reports is different from making up stories," Todd protested.

"Yes, it is," Mr. Bowman agreed. "But the building blocks of any kind of writing are words, and you have a talent for putting them in just the right order. I think you should give this a try. If you're not happy at the end of the week, I'll consider letting you drop the class."

Todd sighed. There were two major games next week—one with John F. Kennedy Middle School, and one with Big Mesa—that he had to practice for. He didn't have time to take a new course, even if it was only for a week. "But, Mr. Bowman—" he began again.

"Todd," Mr. Bowman said, cutting him off. "I'm afraid this discussion is closed. Just try it for a week. See how you feel then."

"Yes, sir," Todd said. "But I already know how I feel," he mumbled as he left the classroom.

Four

"OK, guys, put away your books."

Todd looked up from his English book. It was Tuesday afternoon, and the new teacher had just come into the room. Todd couldn't believe it. The teacher looked young enough to be somebody's older brother. Instead of a suit and tie, he was wearing faded jeans and high-top sneakers.

"I'm Mark Ramirez," the new teacher said. "You can call me Mr. Ramirez." He smiled. "But I'd rather you call me Mark."

Maria, who was sitting behind Todd, gave him a nudge. "He seems pretty cool," she whispered.

Todd shrugged. "Just because he wears high-tops doesn't necessarily make him cool," he said.

Mark looked around the room. Sophia and Amy were still reading their English books. "Stop reading, please," Mark said. Sophia and Amy closed their books. "And put your books away. Your pens and notebooks, too."

There were murmurs in the classroom as the students put their books, notebooks, and pens into their backpacks. "What's he going to do?" Elizabeth whispered to Todd.

"OK," Mark said, rubbing his hands. "Now put your backpacks by the door. You can pick them up on your way out. We've got real work to do."

Todd and Elizabeth exchanged surprised glances. Todd noticed that the other students in the class seemed surprised too, as they dropped their backpacks on the growing pile at the door.

"Great!" Mark said when all the backpacks were gathered at the door. "I want you all to put your chairs in a circle up front." The students grabbed their chairs and formed a circle at the front of the room. Mark joined them. "Let's start by introducing ourselves," he said. "I, as I've already mentioned, am Mark Ramirez." He looked to his right at Amy.

"I'm Amy Sutton," she said.

Patrick Morris introduced himself, then Nora Mercandy. They went around the circle until everyone had been introduced.

"Now that we all know who everybody is," Mark said, "I'd like us to create a story together. The theme will be the choices we make in our lives. Does everybody know what a theme is?"

Elizabeth raised her hand. "The topic of a story?"

Mark nodded and smiled. "Exactly, the topic," he said. "So that means our story is going to be about making choices. I'll start it off."

The class leaned forward. Even Todd couldn't help wondering what was going to happen next.

"Keep in mind," Mark began, "that if our story's about choices, our hero should have to make a choice between two difficult things. Otherwise it's not really much of a choice, OK?"

Everyone nodded.

"All right then, let's begin." He leaned into the circle, his hands on his knees. "Angela played the guitar. She was very good at it and wanted to become a professional musician someday. On Saturday nights, she sometimes played at a small dance club near her home. It was during one of those times that she met David."

He looked at Mandy. "OK, Mandy. It's all yours."

Mandy thought for a moment. "David was tall, dark, and handsome," she said.

Sophia giggled.

"Shh," Mark said, but he smiled at her.

"Soon Angela and David fell in love," Mandy continued. "They thought someday they might even want to get married."

"Your turn, Patrick," Mark said.

Patrick groaned. "How did the story get so mushy already?"

Mark smiled. "You can add whatever you want to, Patrick. If you'd rather not go with the 'mushy' stuff, why don't you tell us something about David? It's his story too."

Patrick brightened. "OK," he said. His forehead wrinkled in thought. Then he smiled. "David was the star quarterback on the high school football team," he said. "He liked football better than anything."

"Except Angela," Mandy added.

Mark smiled. "That's good," he said. "Now, Sophia, what kind of choice will Angela and David have to make?"

"Hmm," Sophia said, thinking. "How about this: Angela needs to practice her guitar on Saturday afternoon for the club, but David wants her to come see him play football."

Mark nodded. "That's good," he said. "But wouldn't David understand that Angela needed to practice?"

Sophia thought about it. "I guess he would."

"So it's not really that hard a choice for Angela to make, right?"

"I guess not," Sophia admitted.

Mark smiled. "Any other ideas?" he asked her.

Sophia shook her head. "Not yet."

"Don't worry," Mark said. "Something will come to you. Anyone else?"

Todd had been sitting back, trying not to get involved. But it was becoming impossible not to. He knew exactly what should happen. Before he could stop himself, he raised his hand.

"Todd?" Mark said.

"How about if David breaks his leg the day of the championship game? Everyone's at the game, and there's no one to visit David in the hospital. He's really upset. It's the championships and he can't be there. He's going crazy, all alone in the hospital. Angela has to make the choice of going to the club and leaving David alone, or staying with him at the hospital."

Mark smiled. "That's pretty good, Todd," he said. "*Very* good, as a matter of fact. The only thing is, Angela's not really giving that much up. I mean, what's one night at the club? She'll just play next week."

Todd nodded. "I see what you mean." He thought for a moment. "How about if there's going to be a big record agent at the club that Saturday night only?" he said. "If Angela plays, it means she might get discovered."

Mark grinned. "That's it!" he said. "*Now* we have a difficult choice. Do you leave someone you love alone and hurting so you can do something you've always wanted to do? Or is love more important than anything else? The choice isn't an easy one, and *that's* what makes a good story."

Suddenly Mark glanced at his watch and stood up. "Well, that's it for today," he said. "I'll see you on Thursday. For next Tuesday's class, I want you all to write a short story of your own."

"How short do you mean?" Mandy asked, looking worried.

Todd was wondering the same thing himself.

Mark laughed. "Don't worry, Mandy. I know you guys have other homework and things to do this weekend. It doesn't have to be long at all—anything over three pages is fine."

"What should we write about?" Randy asked.

"Anything you want. It could be about something you like to do, or an issue that interests you," Mark suggested. "Just make sure your story has a hard choice in it."

Todd looked up at the clock on the classroom wall. He couldn't believe it was three thirty—it seemed impossible that an hour had gone by already. Apparently he wasn't the only one who thought so. A lot of the students seemed reluctant to leave.

"But we still don't know what happened to Angela and David," Elizabeth protested.

"Yeah," Maria agreed. "We didn't get to the end yet."

Mark smiled. "What do *you* think happened, Elizabeth?"

Elizabeth thought about it for a minute. "I think Angela stayed with David in the hospital. There would be other chances to make records, but not to show David how much she loved him."

"That's an excellent ending, Elizabeth," Mark said.

Patrick grimaced. "Yuck," he said. "I'm going to write a story about a solo astronaut. No girls."

Maria frowned at him. "That solo astronaut just might *be* a girl, Patrick," she said.

Mark laughed and clapped his hands. "OK, all of you, shoo. You've been cooped up in school all day. You'll learn a lot more about writing stories out in the world than in any classroom."

"I can't wait to get started," Elizabeth said as she and Todd collected their backpacks and left Mark's class. "I already know what I want to write about: a girl who has to choose between being a mystery writer and a journalist. How about you?"

"I'm not really sure," Todd said. "But I was thinking I might try to write something about basketball."

Elizabeth smiled. "I should have guessed."

As Todd hurried through the locker-room door, Coach Cassels called out, "Wilkins, you're late!"

"Sorry, Coach," Todd said, hurrying to his gym locker. "I lost track of time."

"No excuses!" the coach barked. "Get dressed. Now!"

Todd shoved his backpack into the locker and pulled out his gym shorts and basketball sneakers. He could see he was going to have to rush to get to practice on time on Tuesdays and Thursdays. No more talking after Mark's class. That is, if he continued to *take* Mark's class.

The thing was, the class was a lot of fun, he thought as he changed. He had really enjoyed helping to make up that story. He couldn't wait to start his own.

As soon as Todd made it out to the gym floor,

Peter Jeffries passed him the ball. "Let's see you sink one cold," he challenged.

Todd took the ball down the court and shot a basket. It went straight in, no rim.

"Pretty good, Wilkins," the coach called out. "Now all we have to do is teach you to tell time!"

His teammates laughed, and Todd joined in. Basketball was great. School was great. All in all, life was pretty good.

"Janet almost croaked when I said I couldn't go to the pep rally," Jessica told Elizabeth as they crossed the parking lot at the Valley Mall after school on Wednesday.

"Don't worry, I'm sure she'll recover," Elizabeth said dryly. "You didn't tell her *why* you couldn't go, did you?"

"No way," Jessica said, giving her sister a devilish grin. "I just told her I needed to give a friend *support*."

Elizabeth groaned, but couldn't help smiling. This bra-buying trip was beginning to seem like a real adventure. "Let's make this fast," she said as they entered the mall.

Once inside, they headed straight to Kendall's. They passed the perfume counter and the accessories department, stopping for a second to check out a silver belt that caught Jessica's eye.

"Where's the lingerie department?" Elizabeth asked impatiently as Jessica examined the price tag on the belt.

"Third floor, next to sportswear," Jessica said automatically. Thanks to countless shopping trips with the Unicorns, she knew the layout of every store in the mall. "Why do you think they call it 'lingerie'?"

Elizabeth shrugged. "I don't know. I guess because they can charge more for it than if they just call it underwear."

Jessica giggled. They rode the escalator to the third floor. "There it is!" Elizabeth said, pointing to a sign written in gold curlicue letters.

"Shh!" Jessica said, pushing Elizabeth's hand down. "Do you want the whole *world* to hear you?"

They walked casually toward the lingerie department, pretending to look at the racks of sportswear they passed along the way.

"Come on!" Elizabeth said. She pulled Jessica behind a rack of nightgowns. "This is it!"

Jessica stifled a giggle as she held up a lacy black see-through nightgown.

"Stop fooling around, Jess," Elizabeth said. "Let's hurry up and get this over with." She looked around and spotted the bra section. "Over there!" she said. She pointed to a dozen or so racks full of bras in all colors and sizes.

They gaped at the array of bras. "There are hundreds of them!" Jessica said in dismay. "How do we find the training bras?"

Elizabeth stared at the assortment, then smiled.

"I guess we look for the Dreamlines," she said. "They haven't let us down yet."

The Dreamline bras took up five whole racks. There were lacy ones and satin ones and cotton ones in all colors and sizes. The training bras alone came in five different styles and five different colors. "Now what do we do?" Elizabeth said.

Jessica shrugged. "Try some on, I guess." She picked up a purple satin bra marked 38DD. "Think this one will fit?" she asked Elizabeth, holding it up to her chest.

Elizabeth covered her mouth to keep from giggling. "Only if you wear it as a hat," she said.

Jessica put it on her head. "You know, I think you're right," she said. "And it *is* the official Unicorn color."

Elizabeth couldn't stop herself from laughing. Soon both girls were crouched on the floor, laughing hysterically. "They're going to throw us out of here if you don't quit it, Lizzie," Jessica managed to say at last.

"If *I* don't quit it?" Elizabeth exclaimed. "You're the one putting bras on your head!" That set them off on a whole new laughing fit.

Finally the girls got themselves under control. "Now, come on," Elizabeth said. "This is serious."

Jessica managed to keep a smirk off her face long enough for the two girls each to pick out a couple of bras, all white and in a couple different sizes.

"Let's go try these on," Elizabeth said. "Then we can get out of here, OK?"

"Fine with me," Jessica said. "Where's the dressing room?"

"I think it's over there," Elizabeth said, pointing to a curtained doorway with a saleswoman standing beside it. Elizabeth started walking toward the curtain, but Jessica grabbed her arm.

"Wait!" Jessica said, staring at the saleswoman in horror. "That's Mrs. Hunter, Rick's mother! We don't want her to tell him she saw us!"

Elizabeth looked at the saleswoman more closely. It *was* Mrs. Hunter. And she was starting to look their way! "Quick!" Elizabeth said, pulling Jessica behind a rack of girdles.

They waited a few minutes, then peeked around the girdles to make sure the coast was clear. Then they crept to the Dreamline racks to put the bras back.

"So much for nobody being here," Elizabeth said as they fled toward the escalator.

Five

◇

"How about practicing a few shots after dinner?" Mr. Wilkins asked Todd the next Monday evening.

Todd dragged his fork through his mashed potatoes. "I can't tonight, Dad."

His father looked surprised. "Why not?" he asked. "Are you feeling OK?"

Todd pushed a few peas into his mashed potatoes. "I'm fine," he said. "It's just that I have a lot of homework to do."

"Oh?" his father said. "Maybe I can help you with it."

"No, you can't," Todd said quickly. He didn't want his father to see the basketball story until it was finished. "Uh, I mean, thanks, but I can do it myself. It's not really a big deal; it's just important that I get it done."

His father shrugged. "All right," he said. "But your basketball practice is important too."

Mrs. Wilkins stood up. "Todd practices plenty," she said, starting to clear some plates off the table. "I don't think you have to worry."

Mr. Wilkins got up to help her. "I just don't want him to start slacking off," he said. "When you're finished, son," he told him, "bring your plate into the kitchen. It's your turn to load the dishwasher."

Todd sighed. "I don't have time tonight," he said.

His father frowned. "It's your job."

"I know," Todd said, shoving one last forkful of mashed potatoes into his mouth. "But I have to finish my homework," he mumbled through the potatoes.

His father's eyebrows drew together. "Why do you suddenly have so much homework that you can't practice basketball for half an hour or do your chores?"

Todd bit his lip. He hated to disappoint his father, but he'd been working on his story for Mark every spare moment, and it was taking much longer than he had expected. "It's for the new writing class," he said.

His father put his plate back on the table, his brow still furrowed. "The writing class?" he said, surprised. "But weren't you working on a story for your writing class over the weekend? Did the teacher give you another assignment already?"

Todd shook his head. "No, Dad, it's the same assignment. It's just that it's taking me longer than I thought."

Mr. Wilkins sat down again. "That's a lot of time to spend on one class, son," he said. "After all, you do have other interests. Maybe I should talk to whoever's in charge of assigning this class to you."

Todd gulped down the rest of his milk and thought quickly. Last week he would have loved it if his father had told Mr. Bowman to take him out of the writing class. But now that he had found out how much fun Mark's class was, he didn't want to give it up yet. Especially not before he turned in his basketball story. He liked the way it was turning out, and he wanted to know what Mark would think of it.

"No, Dad," he said hurriedly. "You don't have to talk to Mr. Bowman. I guess I just got carried away and made my story too long. It really only has to be a few pages." Todd almost smiled. He hadn't thought he'd be interested in writing, and now his story was already over ten pages long. "Let's go out and shoot some baskets!"

His father looked a little skeptical. "I don't want you neglecting your studies."

Todd waved his hands. "No problem," he said, forcing a smile. "My story's long enough. I'll just write an ending sentence and it will be done—" he snapped his fingers, "just like that."

His father smiled uncertainly. "Well, if that's really all it needs . . ."

Todd nodded. "Sure. I'll go get my basketball." But as he got up from the table, he was secretly wondering if he'd have enough time that night to finish his story the way he really wanted to finish it.

The only sound on the silent court was the squeak of Tom's sneakers on the gym floor as he aimed the ball at the net. . . .

"Todd!"

Todd jumped in surprise and looked up from his story. He had been so involved in his writing that he hadn't even heard his father open the bedroom door. Now Mr. Wilkins was standing in the doorway, his arms crossed across his chest. "I thought you said that story was finished," he said sternly. "It's past eleven, and you have a game tomorrow. You're going to be exhausted. Get to bed right now."

Todd closed his notebook. He'd been working on his story ever since he'd finished practicing with his father. Tomorrow the basketball team was playing John F. Kennedy Middle School. JFK was a tough team, and Todd really should have gone to bed earlier—he would need to be well-rested for the game.

But he was still having trouble getting the ending just the way he wanted it, and he had to turn the story in tomorrow morning before homeroom. Todd really wanted to finish. He almost had it. Almost . . .

He told his father good night, then turned off his desk lamp and got into bed. Lying in the dark, he waited until his father's footsteps disappeared down the hall. When he heard the door to his parents' bedroom open and close, he threw off the covers, crept over to his desk, and turned the desk lamp back on.

. . . Sweat broke out on Tom's forehead as he let the ball go. If it went in, he would be a hero. If it missed, he would be a loser. But his best friend's father was in the hospital. Tom knew that Jim wanted to shoot the winning shot for his sick dad.

Todd scribbled furiously. He knew what it felt like to want to win. He also knew how it felt to want to please your father and to help out your best friend. His hand flew across the paper, pouring out his feelings. He wrote far into the night.

At breakfast Tuesday morning, Todd could hardly keep his eyes open. He had stayed up until almost three A.M. finishing his story. It had been hard choosing between Tom and Jim.

"Are you feeling OK?" his mother asked him.

"Yes," Todd lied. He was glad his father had gone to work early. He wouldn't want him to worry that Todd wouldn't do well at today's game. Todd was sure he'd wake up once he ate some breakfast.

"Todd!"

He jerked his head up. It was inches from his bowl of oatmeal. "Yes, Mom?"

"Maybe you'd better stay home today," his mother suggested. "You look exhausted."

There was nothing Todd would have liked better than to crawl back into bed. But if he did, he

wouldn't be able to play in the game against JFK—
or attend his writing class, either. "I'm all right," he
told his mother.

She frowned. "You certainly don't look all
right," she said. "Didn't you sleep well last night?"
She reached across the table to feel his forehead.
"Well, you don't have a fever. Still, I think it would
be better—"

Todd sprang up and did a couple of jumping
jacks, forcing a grin onto his face. "I'm fine," he
said. "See?"

"Well, I don't know . . ." his mother said uncertainly.

"I've got to run, Mom, I'm going to be late,"
Todd said, grabbing his backpack off the kitchen
counter. Before his mother could say another word,
he raced off to school.

"This is really exciting," Elizabeth said to Todd
and Maria as they headed to Mark's class later that
afternoon. "I can't wait to hear what Mark thinks of
our stories."

"When I turned mine in this morning I was so
nervous that my hands were shaking," Maria said.

"It took me all night to write mine," Todd said.
"I'm beat."

Maria looked surprised. "Not me. I finished
mine on Sunday," she said. "My philosophy is, the
sooner it's done, the better. Of course, I knew what
I wanted to write about from the very first class."

"So did I," Todd protested. "I started working on it right away too. It's just that it was really hard deciding what the most important choice in the story was."

"Yeah," Elizabeth agreed. "Once you figure out two things that are equally important to someone, it's hard to decide which one is *more* important."

Mark was leaning against his desk when Elizabeth, Maria, and Todd walked into the room. The other students were already in their seats in the circle.

"Good," Mark said, pulling his chair into the circle. "Let's get started."

The class was completely silent. All eyes were on Mark as the students waited to hear what he'd thought of their stories. Elizabeth saw Todd wiping the palms of his hands on his jeans. She gave him an encouraging smile. She was glad to see that he seemed to be taking the writing class seriously, even though he hadn't seemed all that excited about it at first.

Mark pulled out a manila folder. "Let me begin by saying—" The whole class seemed to hold its breath. "—that these stories were all excellent."

Elizabeth glanced at Todd and smiled with relief. He smiled back.

"Now, let's see," Mark said, "where to begin . . ." He shuffled through the papers. "We might as well do this alphabetically," he said, pulling out a story. "Cammi Adams."

Cammi leaned forward in her seat, her chin resting in her hands.

"Cammi did a great job," Mark said. "Her story was about a girl whose parents are deaf . . ." He paused, looking confused, as the rest of the class laughed. "What's so funny about that? Am I missing something?"

Cammi smiled. "It's just that my parents *are* deaf," she explained to the bewildered teacher.

"Ah, I see," Mark said with a smile. "No wonder it seemed so realistic."

"I hope that was OK," Cammi said anxiously. "It's not like cheating or anything, is it?"

"Absolutely not," Mark assured her. "In fact, it's always a good idea to write about what you know, what's important to you."

"Good," Cammi said, looking relieved.

"The details of the parents' lifestyles were excellent, and you really set the scene well," Mark continued. "Your writing was smooth and vivid."

"Way to go, Cammi," Mandy said, giving her a thumbs-up.

Mark nodded. "In fact, the only problem with Cammi's story was one that a lot of the stories had. It was that the choice wasn't really as difficult as, say, our friend Angela's was." He glanced down at Cammi's story. "Cammi's heroine's choice is between staying home to help her parents because the plumber is coming, or going to spend the night at her best friend's house."

"That sounds like a pretty hard choice to me," Maria commented.

"But couldn't her friend come and spend the night at *her* house instead?" Nora argued. "That way everyone would win." She turned to Cammi. "Is that what happens in the story?"

"Not exactly," Cammi said. "Actually, the girl finds out that her aunt is going to be visiting, and that her mother had already asked the aunt to help with the plumber."

Mark nodded. "That's the problem," he said. "The girl didn't really have to make a choice at all, because one of the choices went away."

Cammi shrugged. "I guess that's true," she admitted shyly. "But that's what really happened."

Mark chuckled. "I see. So you really were writing about what you knew—you wrote about something that actually happened!"

"I'm sorry," Cammi said, looking distraught. "I guess I'm not used to making up stories. I thought if I wrote about something true, like I do for the *Sixers*, it would be more interesting."

"Don't apologize!" Mark exclaimed. "Plenty of writers base short stories on things that really happened to them or to people they know. And Cammi, I don't want you to think your story isn't good. It really is. It showed me the way that deaf people live, and the way that some things hearing people take for granted—like dealing with the plumber—can be more complicated." He smiled at her. "I learned something from your story, and that's terrific."

"Thanks, Mark," Cammi said, blushing.

Mark looked down at the pile of papers he was still holding. "Now, let's see . . ." He picked up Pamela's story and went through it the same way, telling the class what it was about and what the best things about it were. But he explained that Pamela's story also needed to show a more difficult choice.

Then he talked about Randy's story and Nora's. He even read parts of Nora's story out loud to the class. She had written a very funny story about a boy who wanted to be a magician, but his tricks kept backfiring. But her story—and Randy's, too— lacked a truly difficult choice.

Mandy's story was next, then Patrick's. Elizabeth was beginning to wish her name came sooner in the alphabet.

"Patrick, you did a fine job," Mark was saying. "Class, his story was about an astronaut named Colonel Murray—" Mark glanced at Maria. "*Not* a girl, by the way." Everyone laughed. "—who has to make a choice between becoming a general and taking an office job, or staying a colonel and continuing on as an astronaut. This had the potential to be a truly difficult choice."

"Thank you, thank you," Patrick said, pretending to take a bow.

Mark laughed along with the class. "The problem was, Patrick said right in the beginning of his story that Colonel Murray didn't care about being a general and that he hated being stuck inside. It would have been better if Colonel Murray *did* want to be a general. That way, the choice would have been more difficult."

Patrick looked a little downhearted. He slumped back into his chair. "Bummer."

"Well, we're zero for six so far," Mandy said. "Mark, did *anyone* get this difficult-choice thing right?"

Mark gave her a mysterious smile. "Well, Mandy, as a matter of fact, one or two of your classmates did write about a truly difficult choice. In fact, the next story, by Julie Porter, was one of them."

"Way to go, Julie," Elizabeth said, giving her friend a smile.

Mark told them about Julie's story. It was about a young musician who had the chance to attend a national music competition. The girl was a senior in high school, so it was her last year to qualify, and after trying for four years she'd finally made it. The only trouble was, the competition was on the same night as the girl's senior prom, and she already had a date with the boy of her dreams.

"It's sort of like the story about Angela and David," Amy commented.

"True," Mark said. "However, this story ends differently. Julie's hero decides that her career in music is more important to her than going to the prom. So she goes to the competition, and wins."

"So it's a happy ending," Mandy said with a smile.

"Well, yes and no," Mark said. "It was happy in

that the girl's career seems to be taking off. But on the other hand, the boy she likes goes to the prom with another girl, and they end up going steady."

"What a drag," Mandy said. She looked at Julie. "Couldn't you have let her win the prize *and* get the guy?"

Mark chuckled. "They can't all have happy endings," he said. "I thought Julie's story was much stronger because she showed that tough choices don't always turn out all good. That's what makes them tough."

Elizabeth nodded. She saw what he meant. She realized that the story she'd written, about a girl who has to decide between accepting a job at a newspaper or trying to write mystery novels, didn't really show that kind of choice.

Sure enough, when Mark got to Elizabeth's story, he told her, "You have a writer's eye for detail. Your story is wonderfully written, and the heroine seems like a real person. But, as I told the others, I would have liked your choice to be more dramatic. After all, even though the girl chooses to take the newspaper job, that doesn't mean she can't quit later to try fiction writing—or that she can't write mystery novels in her spare time."

"I see what you mean," Elizabeth said thoughtfully.

Todd's story was the only one left in the folder. Suddenly Mark looked at his watch. "Todd," he said, "I'm sorry, but it looks like we're out of time. In fact, the class should have ended five minutes ago."

"Oh, no!" Mandy exclaimed. "I'm going to be late for my Unicorn meeting!"

"Oh, no!" Patrick imitated her teasingly. "That's terrible! They may start discussing eyeshadow without you!"

Elizabeth noticed Todd jump up from his seat, his eyes on the clock.

"Todd," Mark called after him. "Could you stay for just a minute? I'd really like to talk to you about your story."

Elizabeth saw Todd nod; his eyes looked worried. *He must be really nervous about his story,* she thought sympathetically as she left the room.

Todd swallowed the lump in his throat. He *was* feeling nervous about Mark's reaction to his story, especially since nobody except Julie really seemed to have gotten the assignment right.

But he was beginning to feel even more nervous about the game that evening. He knew his foul shots still needed some work, and he wasn't sure the coach would understand if he found out the reason Todd hadn't practiced them much that weekend. Todd knew that he should be heading to the gym to put in some last-minute practice right now, but he just had to find out what Mark had thought of his story. Not that he probably thought it was any good. It certainly wasn't as good as Julie's, or Elizabeth's or Cammi's or . . .

"Todd, I just wanted to tell you that out of all the stories I read, yours was one of the very best," Mark said.

Todd looked at him in disbelief. "Are you serious?"

Mark smiled. "The choice your character Tom has to make—whether to sink the winning shot in the game and become a hero, or let his buddy, Jim, do it—is really suspenseful. There's drama and action and a lot of feeling. I think you'll become an excellent writer if you keep working at it."

"You do?" Todd asked, grinning. Then he remembered that the basketball game was starting in less than two hours. There was still time to get in some practice before the game. "I have to go," he told Mark. "But thanks!"

"Keep up the good work," Mark said, as he began putting the circle of chairs back in order.

"I'll try," Todd said, his smile fading. As he left Mark's class, he wondered how he would ever be able to keep playing basketball *and* writing. It was only the third day of writing class, and already he was exhausted.

"Where were you?" Jessica demanded when Elizabeth finally met her in front of school after Mark's class. Jessica was exasperated—they hadn't had another chance to go to Kendall's. Yesterday Elizabeth had had to finish her story for Mark's class, and besides, Jessica had gotten a detention for talking to Ellen during math. Tomorrow she had to go to the dentist after school. Thursday Elizabeth had a field trip to see a play. If they didn't get to Kendall's today, they might never get there!

"I can't believe I'm missing a Unicorn meeting for this," Jessica grumbled as the twins headed toward the mall. "We were supposed to decide whether to have a party if the basketball team makes the district finals, or to wait and have one if they win the championship. Janet is starting to get suspicious about what I'm doing all the time. I'd *much* rather have skipped my dentist appointment tomorrow and gone then."

Elizabeth grinned. "I guess that's just one of life's hard choices, Jess," she said. "Speaking of which, Mark went over our stories today." She smiled. "He said I have a writer's eye."

"That's great," Jessica said, pulling Elizabeth down the walkway, "but I have to be at the basketball game in two hours with the other Boosters, or I'll get the *evil* eye. We've gotta hurry. Let's take the bus."

"I hope this works out better than last time," Elizabeth said as they ran toward the bus stop. "But at least we know Mrs. Hunter won't be there today." She had called the store that morning, and the manager had told her Mrs. Hunter wasn't in on Tuesdays.

Fifteen minutes later, the bus dropped the twins off at the mall. They hurried straight to Kendall's.

Sure enough, the only salesclerk on duty in the lingerie department was a woman they didn't know. "Great!" Elizabeth said. "Come on. But this time, no fooling around."

"Don't worry," Jessica said. "I don't have *time* to fool around today."

The girls once again chose the bras they wanted to try on and brought them to the dressing room. "How many?" the salesclerk asked Elizabeth in a loud, nasal voice.

"Three," Elizabeth said.

The salesclerk gave her a tag. Then she looked at Jessica. "You're twins!" she squawked, as if Elizabeth and Jessica didn't know.

Jessica rolled her eyes at Elizabeth behind the clerk's back. "Uh-huh," she said.

"Isn't that *precious!*" the woman practically screamed. "Getting your first *bras*, girls?"

Jessica and Elizabeth looked at each other, mortified. *Could she say it any louder?* Jessica wondered. "No," she snapped. "Actually, we've been wearing bras for years."

She grabbed the "3 ITEMS" card from the surprised clerk and hurried into the dressing room with Elizabeth right behind her.

"That was pretty embarrassing," Elizabeth said, stepping into one of the stalls. "I thought the whole world would hear her."

"Tell me about it," Jessica replied as she opened the door to the stall to the left of Elizabeth's.

A few minutes later, Jessica was admiring herself in the mirror when she heard voices coming from the dressing room to the left of hers. When she heard Todd Wilkins's name mentioned, she listened more closely. Suddenly she recognized the voice. It was Caroline Pearce, Sweet Valley Middle School's biggest—and least accurate—gossip.

"Anyway, Anita," Caroline was saying, "the game tonight is going to be so much fun. I can't wait."

She must be with her older sister, Anita, Jessica thought.

"Bruce Patman made the winning shot at the last basketball game on an assist from Todd Wilkins. It was the most exciting thing I ever saw."

Jessica rolled her eyes. Was Caroline blind? It had been the other way around—*Bruce* had assisted *Todd.*

"Hey, Jess!" Elizabeth called from the other dressing stall.

Jessica's eyes widened. *Oh, no!* All they needed was for Caroline to find out they were in Kendall's buying bras. She'd tell the whole school in no time. Worse, she'd get it wrong and tell everyone they were buying girdles and see-through nightgowns!

"Shh!" Jessica hissed. She ripped off the bra she'd been trying on, threw her clothes back on, and left the stall. Then she knocked on the door of Elizabeth's. "Are you ready?" she whispered.

Elizabeth opened the door, a bewildered look on her face. "Yes," she said. "What's wrong?"

Jessica pointed to the dressing room to the left of hers.

"And another thing," Caroline was saying loudly, "I heard that Jessica Wakefield got into the creative-writing class, and so did Aaron Dallas."

Elizabeth looked at Jessica. "Caroline *Pearce*?" she mouthed.

Jessica nodded, her eyes wide.

"Let's get out of here!" Elizabeth whispered.

The two girls ran out of the dressing room.

"Did everything fit?" the loud salesclerk asked them.

"Nope, nothing," Jessica said, shoving the bras into her hand.

"Maybe we'll have better luck next time," Elizabeth added, handing her the "3 ITEMS" cards.

The salesclerk stared at them openmouthed. "But these *bras* are on *sale*!" she yelled after them as they ran toward the escalators.

"Just keep going!" Elizabeth muttered to Jessica through clenched teeth.

"I wouldn't stop right now if someone tossed a million dollars at me," Jessica said grimly, jumping onto the escalator behind her twin.

Six

◇

"That was a close one," Peter Jeffries said, towel-drying his hair after the game. "I thought JFK had us there for a while."

Rick Hunter nodded. "Yeah, Wilkins was a little off today. When he missed that last shot, I thought we were goners."

"We're lucky Tim managed a rebound," Peter said. He looked at Tim, who was in front of his locker, tucking in his shirt. "Way to go," Peter told him.

Tim shrugged. "That's why it's called team-work," he said.

Just then Todd came in from the showers, his hair dripping wet.

"What happened out there?" Rick asked him.

Todd shook his head. "I don't know. I just had a bad day, I guess. It happens sometimes."

Tim closed his locker. "That's true," he said. "Still, you know, Wilkins, I don't mean to get on your case, but you looked kind of beat on the floor today."

Rick nodded. "Yeah, by the end of the game you were like the walking dead, man," he said, holding his arms out in front of him like a zombie.

Todd felt like sinking into the ground. He wasn't used to criticism from his teammates. He felt especially bad because he knew they were right, and he knew it was all his fault. He wasn't just having a bad day, he had *caused* himself to have one by spending too much time on that stupid story. "Hey, give me a break," he said defensively, but he was actually feeling more angry at himself than at them.

Just then Coach Cassels came into the locker room. "Wilkins?" he said.

Great, Todd thought. *Like I don't feel bad enough.* "Yes, Coach?"

The coach came over to his locker. "Look," he said. "I know you had an off day, but don't let it get to you, all right? We've got an important game with Big Mesa on Friday, and I don't want one bad game weighing you down." He slapped Todd on the back. "I'd also try getting a little more sleep if I were you."

Todd smiled with relief. The coach was being pretty cool about this. He was actually trying to make Todd feel better. "Sure, Coach," he said. "Sorry about messing up today."

The coach shook his head. "Don't worry about

it," he said. Then his face grew stern. "But I only allow it *once*," he added.

Todd swallowed the lump in his throat. "Right," he said. Then he finished dressing and went out to the gym lobby. The Boosters and about a hundred fans were crowded around Tim.

"Great rebound, Tim!" he heard Winston say.

"The team couldn't have done it without you," Ken added.

Todd sighed. Last week they'd been saying those things to him. He threw his gym bag over his shoulder and looked around for his father. Mr. Wilkins was nowhere in sight, but he saw Elizabeth waving to him from across the lobby. "Hey, Todd!" she called.

"Hi, Elizabeth," Todd said quietly when Elizabeth joined him.

"What's the matter?" she asked.

Todd frowned. "Didn't you see the game?"

"I saw it," Elizabeth said, looking puzzled. "You guys won."

Todd nodded. "No thanks to me."

"What do you mean?" Elizabeth asked. "I thought you played well. You didn't make as many points as you did in the last game, but . . ."

"I know, I know," Todd said. "I was terrible today. I let the team down." He stared at the floor. "It's all because I stayed up all night writing that story for Mark's class. I think I'm going to have to drop it."

"But you can't!" Elizabeth exclaimed. "I saw Mark at the game, and he said your story was great. Besides, the class has that field trip to see a play Thursday."

Todd sighed. "I know," he said, "but we have the Big Mesa game on Friday. I've got to play better than I did today—so I really have to practice on Thursday."

Elizabeth waved the excuse away. "The Big Mesa game's three days away," she said. "You'll have plenty of time to practice on your own before then. You don't want to miss Ryan Stern!"

Todd looked at Elizabeth. She was right. He *didn't* want to miss the chance to see Ryan Stern, his favorite actor, who was starring in the play they were seeing. And he didn't want to drop out of Mark's class. "You're probably right, Elizabeth," he said. "I'll just have to try to get my work done sooner from now on. I'm not going to drop the class."

"I'm glad," Elizabeth said, then she smiled slyly. "Now, when am I going to get to read that great story of yours?"

Todd grinned. "I'll bring it to school tomorrow," he said. "That is, if I can read yours."

"It's a deal," Elizabeth said.

"Todd?" It was Mr. Wilkins. He was making his way through the crowded lobby toward them.

Todd's smile faded at the sound of his father's voice.

"I have to go now," he said to Elizabeth. "I hope

my dad isn't too mad about my messing up today."

Elizabeth glanced over at Mr. Wilkins and then back to Todd. "Don't worry. He'll understand that you just had a bad day." She studied Todd's face. "Won't he?"

Todd shrugged. "I don't know. Basketball is really important to him."

Elizabeth frowned. "I think you should be thinking about what's important to *you*," she said.

"You looked pretty tired out there today," Mr. Wilkins said as they were driving home.

"Dad, we won, and I had five assists," Todd protested.

"Yes, but the team won by only two points. And you missed that last shot after a perfect assist from Peter Jeffries. It almost cost us the game."

"But it didn't," Todd said, slumping down in his seat. "Tim Davis got the rebound. I'm not the only player on the team, you know."

"I know that," his father said. "But your shooting was off. Maybe we'd better spend some time on your jump shot this weekend."

Todd kept his eyes on his lap. After talking to Elizabeth, he had begun to think that maybe he didn't like basketball as much as he used to. Sometimes it seemed as though everybody expected too much from him. His father was making him feel even worse than the guys in the locker room had.

"Coach Cassels said anyone can have an off day," Todd said weakly.

His father glanced at him. "I understand that, Todd, but you're letting other things interfere with your practice, and it's beginning to show."

"I had *one* bad day," Todd insisted. Why was his father picking on him so much? This was the first time Todd had ever let him down!

His father smiled sympathetically. "Look, I don't mean to be rough on you. I just want you to do the best you can do. Isn't that what you want too?"

Todd *did* want to be a good basketball player. He loved the way it felt when he was winning and the crowd was cheering for him. But he also wanted to be a good writer, and to go to the play on Thursday. How was he going to tell his father he needed to miss practice on Thursday now?

He crossed his arms over his chest. He'd just have to find a way. Elizabeth was right. One practice wasn't going to make a difference. He'd *still* do a good job at the Big Mesa game. "I'll do better next time," he told his father. "I promise."

His father smiled. "That's the spirit."

By dinnertime on Tuesday Todd still hadn't figured out a way to tell his father he wanted to go to the play on Thursday. He stared at his meat loaf, trying to come up with an approach.

"Could you please pass the carrots, Todd?" Mrs. Wilkins said.

He figured he could just come right out and *tell* his father, but that probably wasn't the best way. If his father put his foot down, Todd wouldn't be able to go at all. What he had to do was convince his father that going to the play was a good thing. But how?

Mrs. Wilkins cleared her throat. "Todd?"

Maybe if Todd just explained how much he liked Mark's class and how much he was looking forward to the play, his father would understand. After all, Mark had told Todd that his story was one of the best in the class. His father would have to be proud of him if he heard that. Wasn't being good at writing just as impressive as being good at basketball? Todd sighed. *Not to Dad,* he thought miserably.

"Todd, your mother's talking to you," his father said sternly.

Todd glanced up from his meat loaf. "Sorry, what did you say?"

"I asked you to pass the carrots," Mrs. Wilkins said with a slight smile.

"Oh, sure," Todd said, handing her the bowl of string beans.

Mrs. Wilkins shook her head. "The other bowl."

Todd looked at the bowl in his hand. "Sorry." He handed her the carrots.

"Thanks," Mrs. Wilkins said, scooping some carrots onto her plate. She glanced at Todd. "You're awfully distracted tonight, honey. Is something wrong?"

Todd looked at her and took a deep breath. It was now or never—if he didn't settle this now, he never would. "To tell you the truth, I was thinking about my writing class."

"Oh?" Mr. Wilkins asked. He didn't look too happy.

"Yeah," Todd said. He figured the best way to do this was to plunge right in. "It's really a great class. The teacher, Mark Ramirez, is really cool. He wears jeans and high-tops." Todd noticed his father didn't seem very impressed by this. "And he really knows a *lot* about writing. We make up stories in class, and Mark tells us about the best ways to tell a story while we're doing it. Then we write our own."

"That sounds like a lot of fun," his mother said.

"It is," Todd said. "We don't use books or anything."

His father raised his eyebrows. "When I was in school we used books, because teachers should know there's a lot to be learned from books. Has this Mark Ramirez read everything that was ever written? Is that why you don't use books, because he thinks he can just *tell* you everything you need to know?"

Todd gulped. This wasn't going at all the way he'd hoped. "Mark doesn't think he knows everything." He looked helplessly at his mother. "It's just that he thinks you can learn more *outside* school than *inside* it."

Mr. Wilkins put his fork down and stared at

Mrs. Wilkins in disbelief. "Did you hear that? This Ramirez character is teaching the children that school is worthless!"

Todd couldn't believe it. Mark hadn't meant that at all! "That's not true!" he said.

"I think what Todd's teacher probably means is that you can learn certain things from life that you can't learn in school," Mrs. Wilkins explained.

But Mr. Wilkins had that stubborn look he sometimes got on his face, and Todd knew it was hopeless. He'd never be convinced. "He'll learn enough about life when he finishes school," Mr. Wilkins said. "The purpose of school is to teach him things from *books*."

Todd took a deep breath. "Dad, Mark's taking the class on a field trip on Thursday to see a play called *Alternatives*. Ryan Stern is the star. I really want to go."

His father frowned. "You have basketball practice on Thursday and a game on Friday," he pointed out.

"I know," Todd said. "But I can miss one practice. I'll practice extra hard on my own to make up for it." He looked at his mother and his father in turn. "Can I go?"

Mrs. Wilkins glanced at her husband. "It's only one practice, honey. And it sounds like a nice opportunity."

Mr. Wilkins shook his head. "One practice could make all the difference. It could decide whether he wins or loses that game."

"Dad, I'll really, really work hard between now and then," Todd pleaded. "I promise."

Mr. Wilkins sighed. "I'm not going to stop you from going to the play, Todd," he said finally. "That's your choice to make. But I have to go to Sacramento on business Thursday, and Friday I've made arrangements to return to Sweet Valley for the Big Mesa game. I don't want what happened today to happen on Friday."

"Look," Todd said, angry that his father was bringing up today's game again, "I'll be ready."

His father picked up his fork. "Not if you go to that play, you won't."

Seven

"That was great, wasn't it?" Elizabeth said to Todd. It was Thursday after the play, and Mark's students were boarding the bus that would take them back to Sweet Valley.

"It was awesome," Todd replied. He was sitting with Patrick in the seat behind Elizabeth and Amy. "I'd like to try writing a play myself one of these days."

"Maybe one of these days we all will," Mark said, overhearing as he walked past them. He was counting heads to make sure everyone was on the bus. "I took you on this field trip so you could see that there are all kinds of ways to tell a story."

"Brooke Dennis's father writes scripts for Hollywood movies," Elizabeth said. "That's kind of the same as writing a play, isn't it?"

Mark smiled. "Maybe Maria can answer that better than I can," he said.

Maria looked up in surprise.

"I like horror movies," Mark explained. "I saw you in *Mansion of Blood*. You were terrific."

"I haven't made a movie in a long time," Maria said. "It's nice to know I still have some fans."

Maria had been an actress when she was younger. Her parents had moved to Sweet Valley this year to give Maria the chance for a more normal life than she'd had in Hollywood. By now Maria fit in so well at Sweet Valley that it was easy to forget that she had ever been a child star.

Elizabeth looked at Maria and smiled. "So, Ms. Famous Actress," she said, "would you say writing a movie script is the same as writing a play?"

Maria giggled. "Well, it's similar. Only, in movies there are a lot of camera directions and things like that. And there's often more action and less dialogue in a movie than in a play."

"That's probably because in a play you have only a stage to work on and fewer special effects," Patrick said.

Maria nodded. "As a matter of fact, I wouldn't mind taking a stab at scriptwriting myself someday."

"I want to write a mystery novel, like Amanda Howard," Elizabeth said.

"I like creative writing, but I think I like journalism better," Amy said. "I still want to be a newspaper reporter."

Todd leaned forward in his seat. "I'd just like to write short stories," he said.

"You mean you want to be a professional writer now?" Elizabeth exclaimed. "That's great! And just think, you didn't even want to take Mark's class!"

"What about basketball?" Amy added. "I thought you wanted to play professionally someday."

Todd glanced at the two girls, annoyed. "First of all, I didn't say I wanted to be a writer for a *living*," he corrected Elizabeth. "I just said I like to write short stories." He looked at Amy. "And who says I can't play basketball and write, too?"

Amy shrugged, giving Elizabeth a cautious look. "I don't see any problem with doing both."

"I don't either," Elizabeth said.

Todd nodded. "There isn't." But even as he said it, he wondered if that was true.

It was six o'clock when the bus stopped in front of Sweet Valley Middle School. Before the students got out of their seats, Mark clapped his hands for attention. "For your next class, I want you to rewrite your short stories. Pay special attention to the corrections I made, OK, guys?" He gestured toward the bus door. "See you Tuesday!"

I wonder if he wants me to rewrite my story too? Todd wondered as he filed off the bus with the others. Mark had seemed to like his story just the way it was. He hadn't really given him any suggestions for improving it. "Hold on a second, OK?" Todd asked Elizabeth, Maria, and Amy. Maria's mother was picking up all four of them to drive them home. "I have to ask Mark something."

"We'll wait here," Elizabeth said.

Todd ran over to Mark. "Excuse me, Mark?" he said.

Mark put away the notebook he was scribbling in. "What's up, Todd?"

"I was wondering if you want me to rewrite my story too," he said.

Mark scratched his head. "I hadn't thought about that," he said. "Your story's really good as it is." He thought for a moment. "Why don't you write a new story instead?"

Todd's mouth dropped open. "A whole new story?" he said. When was he going to find time to do that—especially with the big game tomorrow night and another the following week?

Mark smiled. "Well, maybe you could just write a new ending for your old story, how does that sound? Look at it from another angle."

Todd breathed a sigh of relief. That sounded a lot more manageable. "You mean like maybe Tom makes the *other* decision?" he asked.

Mark nodded. "Maybe," he said. "Or maybe you can invent a whole different choice that Tom has to make."

Todd nodded. "OK. I'll see you Tuesday!"

"This is it, team," Coach Cassels said the following evening, looking at each of the Gladiators in turn. His eyes seemed to linger a little longer on Todd. It was Friday afternoon, and the Sweet Valley Middle School Gladiators were playing Big Mesa. Coach Cassels had just called the final time-out, stopping the clock above the backboard at ten seconds. The Gladiators were down by one point.

"Todd and Tim, you're our best shooters," Coach Cassels continued. "I want you two to take the ball down the court. This is our last chance. If we miss this shot, you can kiss our winning streak good-bye. Got it?"

"Sure, Coach," Todd said.

"Got it," Tim said, giving Todd the thumbs-up.

When the referee blew the whistle, Tim and Todd started to bring the ball down the court. Todd passed it to Tim, and Tim passed it back. They were getting close to the net. The crowd was roaring. The Boosters' pom-poms were waving wildly.

Todd passed the ball to Tim. Two Big Mesa players closed in on Tim, trying to steal the ball. Todd glanced at the clock. Five seconds left in the game.

Tim passed the ball to Todd just before one of the Big Mesa players tried to steal it. Three seconds left. Todd was open for the final shot.

A Big Mesa player came charging at him, trying to stop him. Todd took aim. The crowd rose to their feet. Someone started chanting, "Wil-kins, Wil-kins, Wil-kins," and soon all the Gladiator fans picked up the chant. Todd was soaked with sweat.

Two seconds. He measured the distance from the basket, aimed, and shot.

The ball hit the backboard. It hovered on the rim. *Go in, go in,* Todd prayed. The ball circled and circled the rim. The gym was silent, as if the whole crowd was holding its breath.

Finally the ball tipped to the outside of the rim and fell to the ground.

There were cheers on the Big Mesa side of the gym, groans on the Sweet Valley side. The buzzer sounded, signaling the end of the game. The Gladiators had lost their first game of the season.

And it was all Todd's fault.

The locker room was like a tomb as the Gladiators changed out of their uniforms into their regular clothes. "If you hadn't missed practice yesterday," Peter snapped at Todd, "we wouldn't have lost."

No one else said anything. Todd knew the rest of the team blamed him too. He didn't try to defend himself. They were right. He'd felt it from the start of the game. Something was off. He wasn't as limber as usual, and the moves didn't come as easily as they did when he was in top condition. His father had been right—that one missed practice *had* made the difference between winning and losing.

When Coach Cassels came into the locker room, Todd was sure he was going to tell him that he was off the team. But the coach didn't even look at Todd. He looked around at the rest of the boys, his face stern. "We should have had better defense around Todd and Tim," he said. "Big Mesa was bearing down too hard."

Peter made a disgusted face. "Todd shouldn't have missed that shot," he muttered.

Coach Cassels glared at him. "Basketball players don't talk about their teammates like that," he warned Peter.

But Todd noticed that the coach didn't say that Peter was wrong about Todd's missing the shot. He looked at Todd. "Be at the next practice," he said coldly. "On time."

"Yes, sir," Todd said, wishing he could disappear into the ground. After the coach left, Todd looked around at his teammates. "I'm sorry," he said. "Peter's right. I should have made that shot."

"Hey, don't sweat it," Tim said. "You win some, you lose some."

"That's right," Rick said, giving Todd a slap on the back. "Don't let it get you down, Wilkins."

Several of the other boys added their reassurances, but not all of them sounded as though they really meant it.

Todd sighed and rolled up his knee pads. He couldn't help what the others thought of him. He'd just have to be sure to do better next time. He finished dressing quickly and left the locker room.

The gym lobby was almost completely deserted—except for Todd's father. He was standing just inside the door, his arms crossed. He looked upset.

"I warned you, Todd," Mr. Wilkins said as he and Todd headed for the car. "If you'd gone to practice yesterday, this never would have happened." He shook his head. "You should have taken my advice, but you ignored me and went to that play instead."

Todd was getting sick of everyone blaming the lost game on him. Maybe it *was* his fault, but did he have to hear it over and over and over again? "I was nervous," he said. "Even if I'd gone to practice yesterday, I still would have been nervous. The coach practically put the whole game on Tim and me."

His father shook his head. "It wasn't just nerves," he said. "You're slipping. I can tell just watching you on the court. You're spending too much time writing and not enough time on your basketball practice. That teacher of yours—what's his name—is giving you too much work."

"But Mark *isn't* giving me too much work," Todd protested as they climbed into the car. "I *like* writ—"

"Don't defend him," his father interrupted. "It's

not fair to expect that much extra time of kids who are involved in other activities."

They drove in silence for a while. "You and I are going to do some serious practicing this weekend," his father said finally.

"But—"

"No excuses," his father said. "You've got to be in good shape for next week's game."

"All right, but I've got a lot of other stuff I have to do this weekend," Todd said.

His father parked the car, then looked at him. "What kind of 'stuff'?" he demanded.

"Homework," Todd said weakly.

"Your homework never interfered with your basketball practice before," his father said. He turned off the ignition and faced Todd, his expression serious. "Todd, I really think you should consider dropping that class."

"But, Dad—"

"I'm telling you this for your own good, son," Mr. Wilkins said grimly. "That class is going to ruin your chance to make something of yourself. It's just not worth it." He gave a short little laugh. "Especially when it's being taught by a teacher who doesn't believe in using books."

"He doesn't—" Todd began.

"I've said all I have to say on this matter. I won't sit back and watch you flush your hopes for a basketball career down the toilet. I want you to give up that class, and I mean it."

Todd watched his father get out of the car and slam the door behind him. He sat in the dark car a while longer, trying to figure out what to do.

The only thing *to* do, he finally decided, was to go and talk to Mark first thing tomorrow morning. As much as he hated to do it, he was just going to have to quit the class.

Eight

◇

The sound of rain pounding on her window awakened Elizabeth Saturday morning. "Rain?" she mumbled, her eyes half open. Then she remembered it was Saturday. Darn. She hated when it rained on a Saturday.

She got up and went to the window. Puddles pooled on the walkway, and raindrops dripped from bushes and trees. She sighed. There was nothing to do but stay inside until it stopped. Even the mall would probably be deserted in a storm like this.

The mall!

She glanced at the clock radio beside her bed. It was eight forty-five. The mall opened at nine thirty. If it kept raining for another hour, which it looked as though it was going to, they'd have Kendall's practically all to themselves!

She hurried through the bathroom to Jessica's bedroom. "Wake up!" she commanded, shaking Jessica by the shoulder.

Jessica turned over groggily. "Time for school already?" she mumbled, opening one eye.

Elizabeth shook her head. "It's Saturday."

Jessica glared at her through her one open eye. "Why are you waking me up this early on a Saturday?" she demanded, rolling over and pulling a pillow over her head.

Elizabeth shook her again. "Come on, get up! It's raining out!"

Jessica rolled over onto her back and pushed the pillow away, looking at Elizabeth as if she'd lost her mind. "Why would I want to get up on a rainy Saturday?" She tossed the pillow at Elizabeth. "Go away."

Elizabeth put her hands on her hips. "Come on, Jess. No one will be out this morning. It's the perfect time to buy our bras!"

Jessica sat up and pushed a strand of hair out of her eyes. "What *are* you talking about?"

Elizabeth sighed. "It's pouring out. No one will want to go out until the rain stops. If we go to Kendall's now, nobody will be there."

Jessica's eyes widened. "Oh, I get it! Good thinking!"

Elizabeth tossed the pillow back at her sister. "Thanks. I know."

*   *   *

There was hardly anyone in the mall when Elizabeth and Jessica arrived. They shook out their umbrellas, then headed for Kendall's.

"This is great!" Jessica said. "It's like they opened the mall especially for us!" She gazed around at the nearly empty stores they were passing.

As the twins entered the department store, they both gasped. "Look at that!" Jessica said.

"Wow!" Elizabeth breathed. "It looks like one of Lila Fowler's parties!"

"Better!" Jessica said, staring at the balloons and streamers that were strung everywhere in and around Kendall's. A huge banner across the front door announced "WELCOME TO KENDALL'S ONE MILLIONTH AND ONE SALE!" There were smaller signs proclaiming, "Today Only! Half-Price Sale!"

Elizabeth looked at Jessica. "This is awesome!" she said. "Not only is no one here, but they're having a big sale, too. That means we can get two bras each!"

Giggling, the twins headed toward the escalator. As they passed the perfume counter, a saleswoman dressed in a blue satin evening gown and dangling diamond earrings burst into a grin. "Can I interest you girls in some perfume?" she asked. "It's on sale."

Elizabeth shook her head. "We, um, have to go to the third floor for something."

The clerk looked disappointed.

Another saleswoman, dressed in a pink taffeta

dress, called out to them from accessories as they walked by. "We've got a great deal on scarves today, girls!" she said sweetly. She hurried over to Elizabeth with a blue and green scarf. "Now, doesn't that look just lovely with her eyes!" she said to Jessica, holding the scarf against Elizabeth's cheek. Then she did a double take. "Twins!" she said. "Well, let me see if I have another scarf for you, dear."

While she was looking for a second scarf, the twins sneaked off to the escalator. "The salespeople must have had a pep talk or something this morning," Jessica said.

Elizabeth nodded. "It's like we're the last customers on earth."

"It's sort of depressing," Jessica said. "They're having this huge celebration and the store's deserted."

When they reached the third floor, they scooted past a salesman dressed in a tuxedo who tried to sell them some men's ties, and ran to the lingerie department. "Let's just hurry up and buy our bras before they try to sell us the *store*," Elizabeth said, giggling.

They went over to the Dreamline bras rack and picked out the bras they'd tried on the last time they were at Kendall's.

"Would you like to try those on?" the saleswoman with the loud mouth asked. Today she was wearing a black sequined dress and black sparkling earrings. It looked strange at this hour in the morning.

Elizabeth and Jessica glanced at each other. "No, thank you," they said in unison.

"We already know they fit," Elizabeth added. "We'd just like to pay for them." *And get out of this store before anything embarrassing happens,* she thought.

The salesclerk grinned. "Well, that's just *great!*" she practically screamed, grabbing the bras out of their hands. "Come right over to this register—" She glanced toward the dressing rooms. "—and I'll *ring* these *sales* right *up!*"

Elizabeth covered her ears.

"What's she shouting for?" Jessica whispered angrily. "She's even louder than before!"

Elizabeth shrugged. "I have no idea."

Suddenly a swarm of people, dressed as though they were going to a ball, descended on the lingerie department. Cameras started clicking. The lingerie saleswoman posed, holding the twins' bras out in front of her with a big smile on her face. "Welcome, one millionth and one customers!" shouted a man with gray hair and a gray mustache, dressed in a gray pinstripe suit. He flashed the twins a big smile. "As president of Kendall's, let me be the first to congratulate you! Not only will you receive a ten-percent discount on all your Kendall's purchases for the next year, but your pictures will be used in *every one of our ads*, too!"

"Really?" Jessica exclaimed, reaching her hand up to fix her hair.

"Oh, no!" Elizabeth exclaimed as the cameras started flashing. "Run, Jess!" Elizabeth grabbed Jessica's arm and dragged her out of the lingerie department toward the escalator.

"What are you doing?" Jessica demanded as her sister raced down the escalator, still clutching her arm. "They wanted us to be models!"

Elizabeth rolled her eyes. "Think about it, Jess. Pictures of ourselves buying *bras* plastered all over every Kendall's flyer for an entire year!"

Jessica shuddered. "Oh, I didn't think of that. I guess you're right."

They stopped in the parking lot to catch their breath.

Elizabeth was shaking her head in disbelief. "Why is buying two dumb bras turning into such a nightmare?"

Jessica couldn't help laughing. "Maybe we should have just talked to Mom."

Todd got to school early Monday morning, before any of the other students had arrived. He hurried down the hall to Mark's office and knocked on the door.

"Come in," Mark called. When he saw who it was, his face broke into a smile. "Hey, Todd. What can I do for you this morning?"

Todd stepped into the room and closed the door behind him. "Um, hi, Mark. I need to talk to you about something. It's kind of important."

Mark set aside the papers he was correcting. "Have a seat," he said, gesturing to the chair beside his desk.

Todd sat down and cleared his throat. Now that he was here, he wasn't sure what to say.

"So, what's up?" Mark asked, leaning back in his chair and crossing his feet on the desk.

Todd sighed. He stared at his hands for a moment. "I'm going to have to drop your class." He couldn't bring himself to look at Mark. He hoped Mark would just tell him it was all right, so he wouldn't have to explain.

"Drop my class?" Mark took his feet off the desk and leaned forward. "Why? I thought you enjoyed writing."

Todd forced himself to meet Mark's gaze. "I do. But it's taking up too much of my time. It's interfering with . . . other things."

Mark looked confused. "What other things?"

"Well," Todd said hesitantly. "Basketball. I've missed a couple of practices since this class started, and it's showing in my game."

"Oh," Mark said.

Todd looked at Mark helplessly. "I'm really sorry, but I don't have any choice."

Mark raised his eyebrows. "But you made a choice, didn't you? If there's one thing I've been trying to teach you guys, it's that everyone has to make tough choices all the time. Your choice was between basketball and writing, and basketball won. Isn't that right?"

Todd shook his head. "No, this isn't what I *wanted* to do at all. I really wanted to do both. But I was letting too many people down."

Mark looked surprised. "Hold on a second, Todd. I'm not getting this. If you want to keep writing, why don't you? If there's a problem with your writing and basketball, maybe I can talk to Coach Cassels—"

"No!" Todd said. He dropped his gaze to the desk. "I mean . . . well . . . the coach has been pretty cool about the whole thing, considering. It's my father who's the real problem. He really wants me to quit so I can concentrate more on basketball. He pretty much ordered me to drop out after I missed an important shot in the last game."

Mark sat back in his chair. "Oh," he said. "It's your *father* who thinks writing is interfering with your basketball."

Todd nodded. "See, he used to be a star basketball player in high school, and then he injured his knee and couldn't play anymore."

"So he wants you to play basketball as well as he did," Mark said.

"Yeah. He thinks I'm not spending enough time practicing because I'm spending too much time writing."

"I understand," Mark said, a thoughtful expression in his eyes. "You know what? My dad wanted me to be a football player."

Todd looked up. "Really?"

Mark smiled. "Sure. I have a pretty good arm, and I'm reasonably fast. My dad wasn't any too pleased when I decided I wanted to be a teacher instead."

Todd's eyes widened. "But you're a great teacher!"

Mark grinned. "Thanks. And you're a great writer."

Todd's gaze dropped back to the desk. "I can't just ignore what my dad says," he said quietly.

Mark sighed. "You know, Todd, I'm sure your father only wants what's best for you. My father thought he was doing what was best for me when he tried to make me go to a college with a good football team instead of one with a good English department. But you can't always let someone else make your choices for you."

Todd looked at him, unsure of what to say.

"Tell me something, Todd," Mark continued. "Do *you* think you're spending too much time writing and not enough time practicing?"

Todd shrugged. "I guess so. I mean, I shouldn't have missed that final shot yesterday. I was pretty nervous and everything. And it wasn't that hard a shot."

"No, that's not what I mean," Mark said. "When you're writing, would you rather be practicing basketball?"

Todd thought about it a minute. Finally he shrugged. "I don't know," he said hopelessly. "Not really. But I do want to be at my best on the court."

Mark sighed. "I'm not going to lie to you, Todd. You already know how I feel about your writing. I think you have a lot of talent, and I think you add a lot to the class. *And* I think there might be room for both writing and basketball in your life." He rested his elbows on the table. "I know this is tough on you," he continued. "But I'm afraid I can't make it any easier. I don't know if dropping my class is the right choice. Only *you* can decide that." His eyes met Todd's. "You know, Todd, one of the most important parts of growing up is having the courage to be your own person. That's about the best advice I can give you."

Todd got up from the chair. "Thanks," he said quietly. "I guess I have some more thinking to do about this whole thing."

Mark walked him to the door. "I'd really like you to stay in the class, Todd, but I'll understand either way. Let me know what your decision is, OK?"

Todd nodded. "If I can ever *make* a decision," he said as he left the room.

"Are you OK?" Elizabeth's voice broke through Todd's thoughts as he left Mark's classroom. It was already eight thirty, and the corridor was filled with students.

He shrugged. "I don't know."

"What happened?" Elizabeth asked.

Todd lifted his hands helplessly. "I'm not sure. I just went to see Mark because my father told me to quit the writing class. He said Mark gives us too much work, and that's why my basketball game has been off lately."

"Oh, no!" Elizabeth exclaimed. "What did Mark say?"

"He asked me if that's what I wanted to do. If it was my choice."

Elizabeth nodded. "What did you tell him?"

"I told him I didn't know," Todd said.

Elizabeth looked at him sympathetically. "Mark's right. It should be your choice." She touched his arm. "I know it's hard to make those kinds of decisions. Take me, for instance. When we first started middle school there was nothing Jessica would have liked better than for me to join the Unicorns. At first I gave it a try because I wanted her to be happy, but I found out I just wasn't interested in what the Unicorns are interested in. I love Jessica, but I couldn't go against my own feelings. She was upset about it at first, but she came around because she realized I was just doing what I knew I had to do."

Todd nodded. "But my situation is different. Part of me wants one thing and part of me wants another."

"I see what you mean," Elizabeth said, shrugging helplessly. "That makes it much harder. But I just know it's important to be what *you* want to be, no matter what anyone else wants."

Todd searched her eyes. "I know. I wish I knew what that was."

Nine

The only sound on the silent court was the basketball slowly circling the rim, Todd wrote. *It circled and circled as the players watched it, frozen. Tom was torn between wanting to sink the winning shot so the team could go to the championships, and wanting the ball to miss so he could enter the photography contest. Tom hadn't told his father yet that he wanted to be a photographer.*

It was so quiet in the gym that Tom could practically hear the sweat breaking out on his forehead. Then the fans began to roar as the ball went in.

Tom breathed a sigh of relief. He was happy for the team. Now they could go to the championships. But in that breathless moment when he was waiting for the ball to sink or miss, he had realized something: He had been waiting for the ball to make his decision for him—if it went in, he played basketball; if it missed, he entered the contest. At the last second, he realized that that was a cop-out. He must make the decision himself. The team deserved to go to the championships. And Tom deserved to see if he was good enough to be a photographer.

The team carried him off the court on their shoulders. It was one of the greatest feelings he'd ever had. But as much as he relished the moment, the team would have to go to the championships without him this time. He had made the decision to enter the contest instead. The End.

Todd ripped the last sheet of paper from his notebook and read over what he had just written. "Todd, dinner's ready!" his mother called.

Todd drew a deep breath. *This is it*, he thought as he glanced at his story one last time. *Tonight I tell Dad that I'm not going to quit Mark's class.*

Todd waited until his father had started eating before he nervously cleared his throat. "Dad?" he said.

"Yes, Todd?" said Mr. Wilkins, scooping up a forkful of pasta salad.

Todd screwed up his courage. "I talked to Mark Ramirez today."

Mr. Wilkins put his fork back down. "Oh?"

"I decided I'm not going to quit the writing class."

Mr. Wilkins's eyebrows came together angrily. "What do you mean?" he demanded. "After everything we talked about, after those two disastrous games . . ."

Todd glanced desperately at his mother for help.

"Why don't you let Todd tell his side of the story?" Mrs. Wilkins suggested quietly but firmly.

"Fine." Mr. Wilkins turned and looked at Todd expectantly.

"Well, um, I went to Mark's office today to tell him that I was quitting the class," he began nervously. "But Mark made me realize I don't really *want* to quit the class. I was only quitting it because *you* want me to."

"Yes, I do," Mr. Wilkins said, "and I'm your father."

Todd took a deep breath. "I know that," he said. "And I'm not trying to disobey you. But I'm twelve years old. Sooner or later I have to start making my own decisions." He looked at his mother, who nodded encouragingly. "I've decided I don't want to quit Mark's class."

His father sat back in his chair and crossed his arms. His eyebrows were still drawn together angrily. "Todd," he said at last, "I appreciate your need to make your own decisions. I *want* you to do that. It's part of growing up. However, I don't think quitting writing class *is* your decision. I think this teacher—Mark—is influencing you entirely too much. Encouraging you to disobey your parents is the last thing a teacher should do."

"But, Dad—"

"The fact is, you have the ability to be a star basketball player, and Mark Ramirez is telling you to throw it away!"

"Dad, Mark wants me to—" Todd began, wanting to explain that Mark would want him to give up writing if that was what *Todd* really wanted to do.

"I don't care what Mark wants you to do!" Mr. Wilkins snapped. He ran a hand through his hair. "Do you know what it felt like when my knees went?" he said. "I thought I was going to be able to play basketball forever. I missed the championship game my junior year of high school because my parents were taking a trip to Hawaii and I wanted to go with them. The next year, I fell and injured my knee during practice." He stared at his hands. "I never made it to another championship game."

Todd felt terrible. He didn't know what to say.

His father shook his head. Suddenly he looked very old and tired. "There's nothing you can tell me that I don't already know," he said, getting up from the table. "When you finish your dinner, I want you to go to your bedroom and think about what I've told you."

Before Todd could say another word, Mr. Wilkins left the room.

Todd sat on his bed, staring at the version of his story that he had finished just before dinner. He'd been up in his room thinking for an hour now, and still nothing made sense.

He carried the story to his desk and opened his notebook. First he crossed out "The End." Then he took a fresh piece of paper.

The team would go to the championships without Tom this time. At least, that's what he'd thought when the buzzer sounded and the team carried him off the court on their shoulders. But back in the locker room, listening to the guys joke together and talk about the game, he began to realize he'd miss the team. He'd miss basketball. He didn't know what to do.

On the way home from the game with his father, Tom finally told him what the problem was. "I want to be a photographer, Dad," Tom said. "But I also want to play basketball."

His father nodded and put a hand on Tom's shoulder. "Tom, you have to make your own decisions. I can't do that for you. But let me tell you a story."

Tom sat back in the passenger seat, watching his father intently.

"When I was your age," Tom's father said, "I was as good a basketball player as you are."

Tom looked surprised. His father had limped for as long as Tom could remember. He couldn't imagine his dad jumping around on a basketball court.

"The limp was a basketball injury. I never told you because I didn't want you to feel you had to play basketball for my sake. I wanted you to do it because you loved the game."

Tom nodded. "I do love it. But I love photography, too."

His father patted his shoulder. "I understand, son," he said.

Todd stared at what he had written. So what would Tom do now? Go to the contest? Play basketball? He tore the page from his notebook and crumpled it up. How could his character make a decision when he couldn't even make a decision himself?

He threw himself onto his bed and covered his head with a pillow. *What am I going to do?*

Ten

◇

Todd was on his way down to breakfast Tuesday morning when he heard his mother and father talking in the kitchen.

"I made an appointment with Mr. Clark this morning to talk about Mark Ramirez, so I'll be going to the office late today," his father was saying.

"Are you sure that's a good idea?" Mrs. Wilkins asked.

"It has to be done," Mr. Wilkins replied. "I'm going to straighten this thing out once and for all."

Todd felt his heart plummet. He rushed into the kitchen, and both his parents looked up in surprise. "You can't do that!" Todd said. "Mark didn't do anything wrong!"

Mr. Wilkins shook his head. "I'm sorry, but that's not for you to decide, son." He glanced at his watch. "I'm leaving in fifteen minutes. If you want a ride, I'd be happy to take you."

Todd stared at his feet. What he wanted was to disappear forever. "No, thanks," he said stonily. "I'll walk."

Todd waited in his room until his father had left the house. Then he went downstairs for breakfast. "Why is he trying to get Mark fired?" he asked his mother miserably as he poured cereal into a bowl. "Mark didn't do anything wrong."

Mrs. Wilkins sat beside Todd. Her forehead was wrinkled with concern. "Todd," she said, "I know it's hard for you to understand right now, but your father thinks he's doing what's best for you. He's worried that Mark Ramirez is a bad influence."

"But he's not!" Todd protested. "All the students like him. He's one of the best teachers I've ever had."

Mrs. Wilkins frowned uncertainly. "He does seem to give you an awful lot of work, Todd. And he did talk you into going against your father's wishes."

Todd pushed his cereal away. "No, he didn't! He just said I should make my own decisions. And he's right!" He got up and cleared away his cereal bowl, untouched.

"Todd, please try to understand," Mrs. Wilkins said. "Your father is only doing this because he loves you."

"Then I wish he'd love me a little less," Todd

snapped, taking his backpack from the kitchen counter.

His mother shook her head. "No, you don't, Todd." She stood up and gave him a hug. "Everything will work out, you'll see."

"Sure," Todd said. But the way he saw it, nothing was working out at all.

"Is everything OK, Todd?" Elizabeth asked Todd anxiously that morning, hurrying over to his locker.

Maria came up a second later. "Todd, what's going on? I saw your father going into Mr. Clark's office this morning."

Todd felt himself turn red. He pretended to look for something in his locker.

"What happened?" Patrick said, walking over. "Did you cut class or something? I saw your father coming out of Mr. Clark's office a while ago."

Todd sighed. What was the deal? Had everyone in the whole school seen his father that morning? He knew he couldn't stall forever. But he couldn't bring himself to tell his friends the truth, either. "Um, it has something to do with basketball practice," he said.

"Then shouldn't he be talking to Coach Cassels?" Patrick asked.

Todd gulped. "I don't know."

Maria looked surprised. "Didn't you ask him?"

Todd shrugged. "I was, um, running late."

Elizabeth looked questioningly at Todd. "Listen, if there's anything I can do to help," she began.

"Yes," Maria agreed. "We're all your friends, Todd."

Todd slammed his locker door shut. "Look, this is my problem, OK? So just leave me alone!"

Elizabeth's mouth dropped open. She looked at Maria and Patrick, who seemed as surprised as she was. "We didn't mean anything," Elizabeth said, looking a little hurt.

Todd's shoulders drooped. His friends were only trying to help. He was especially ashamed of snapping at Elizabeth when she was only trying to be nice. "I know," he said. "I'm sorry. But I'd rather not talk about it now, all right?"

"All right," Elizabeth said, looking down. Finally she glanced up and met his gaze. He could read the concern in her eyes. "But if you do want to talk about it, let me know, OK?"

Todd sighed. "I know. Thanks. But right now I just need to be by myself for a while."

"We're here for you too, Todd," Maria added, and Patrick nodded.

"Thanks," Todd said. But he wondered how they'd feel if they knew what his father was *really* up to.

Todd went straight to his room after school. *This whole thing is turning into a nightmare,* he thought as he lay on his bed, staring at the ceiling. The only good thing about it was that it couldn't get any worse.

"Todd, dinner!" his father called.

Todd sighed and pushed himself off the bed. He wasn't very hungry, but if he didn't go down to dinner, his father would think he was being stubborn. The last thing he needed was for his father to find something else to lecture him about. Besides, he had to find out what had happened at school between Mr. Clark and his father. He had to know if his father had gotten Mark fired.

When his father didn't bring up the topic after a few minutes, Todd cautiously asked, "So what happened with you and Mr. Clark today?"

"Nothing," Mr. Wilkins said, a frustrated expression on his face. "Mr. Clark thinks the world of Mark Ramirez."

Todd took a deep breath. He was overwhelmed by relief. Mark hadn't been fired! If Todd practiced his basketball really hard and played really well at the next game, maybe his father would forget all about the whole thing. "I'm going to go out and shoot some baskets after dinner," he told his father. "Want to come?"

His father smiled, but Todd noticed that he seemed a little distracted. "I'm sorry, Todd," he said. "I have some phone calls I have to make tonight."

"That's OK," Todd said. "Maybe tomorrow." He ate two helpings of the spaghetti and meatballs his mother had made. He felt better than he had in a long time. Everything was going to work out after all.

"Alice? This is John Wilkins, Todd's father. Yes, fine, thanks. How are you?"

Todd had just come in from practicing basketball in his driveway when he overheard his father talking on the phone in the den. *Alice is Elizabeth's mother's first name. But why would he be calling Mrs. Wakefield?* Todd wondered. He couldn't resist pausing outside the door to listen.

"Listen, I understand Elizabeth is taking a writing class with a teacher named Mark Ramirez."

Todd nearly dropped his basketball. Why was his father talking to Mrs. Wakefield about Mark?

"The reason I'm calling you," Todd's father continued, "is that Todd's been having some problems with this writing class. Mr. Ramirez has been giving Todd so much work that he's been unable to keep up with his other activities." Todd heard his father drop his voice. "And I'm afraid he's encouraged Todd to disobey my wishes."

Todd listened in horror. He wanted to run into the den, to tell him it wasn't true. But he knew it wouldn't make any difference. He'd only get Mark in more trouble.

"Yes, Alice, I did talk to Mr. Clark about it," his father continued after a pause. "I talked to him this morning, as a matter of fact. But he refused to do anything about the problem. That's why I'm calling you. I'm calling the Suttons, the Porters, the Jacobsons, and some of the other parents as well. If Mr. Clark won't take care of this problem, we'll have to take care of it ourselves."

Todd gnawed on his thumbnail. What did his father mean, "take care of it ourselves"?

"Thank you, Alice," Mr. Wilkins said. "I knew I could count on your support. I'll be in touch." He hung up the phone.

Todd ran to his room before his father caught him listening. This was horrible! Just when he thought it was all over, it had suddenly gotten worse than he ever could have imagined. His father was turning all the other parents against Mark too! And it was all because Todd had messed up a couple of times playing basketball!

Todd paced his room. Finally he went to his desk and opened his notebook. If he could write about this, maybe he could figure out what to do.

He stared at the blank page, his pen in his hand. But after half an hour of staring, the page was still blank. He put his notebook away and lay down on his bed. He didn't know what to do now. He would just have to wait to see what happened.

"What's going on, Todd?" Pamela Jacobson demanded as soon as Todd reached his locker on Wednesday morning. Her blue-gray eyes flashed with anger. "My mom says your father's trying to get Mark fired because *you* made the basketball team lose the game with Big Mesa!"

Todd couldn't believe it. Several of the kids from the writing class were waiting in front of his locker for him. "That's not it at all—" he began. "I never said—"

"Where did your father get an idea like that if it wasn't from you?" Sophia demanded.

Maria shook her head. "You told us your father was going to see Mr. Clark about basketball practice."

Todd dropped his head. "It *was* about basketball practice," he said. "Kind of."

"Come on, Todd," Patrick said angrily. "It *was* about you missing basketball practice. But that wasn't Mark's fault, that was your fault. You were the one who decided to miss practice."

"I know that," Todd said helplessly. "I tried to tell my father—"

"You obviously didn't try very hard," Pamela snapped, tossing her wavy brown hair over her shoulders.

"Now all our parents think Mark is a bad teacher," Amy said. "Mr. Clark might have to fire him."

Todd wished a hole would open up in the ground and swallow him. Then he saw Elizabeth walking down the hallway. Elizabeth would understand. "Elizabeth!" he called.

Elizabeth stopped in front of him, clearly upset. "You made *your* decision," she said quietly, "but it doesn't mean you should make it for the rest of us. This class means a lot to some people, you know."

Todd couldn't believe it. Even Elizabeth thought he was trying to get Mark fired. He looked from one of his classmates to the other. Then, without a word, he turned and walked away.

He didn't know exactly where he was going. All he knew was that he couldn't face his friends, and he especially couldn't face Mark. He didn't even think as he left the school grounds, heading toward Secca Lake. He just knew he needed time to clear his head. He'd never been in a worse situation than this in his life. And the worst part was that he couldn't think of anything that could possibly make it better.

He sat beside the lake all morning, staring at the clear blue water. He wished he could stay there forever. But he knew he was only putting off what had to be done. Sooner or later he would have to face his classmates. And Mark.

He got up and started walking home. On his way, he saw some little kids playing basketball in the Sweet Valley Elementary schoolyard. He stopped for a few minutes and watched them through the chain-link fence. They all seemed so happy and carefree. They were having so much fun. It seemed like such a long time ago that he'd had fun playing basketball. When had everything gone wrong? He sighed. He knew the answer: It had all gone wrong when he had started the writing class.

He continued on his way home. When he got there, he sneaked inside and hurried straight up to his room. He didn't want to have to see his mom and explain why he was home early. He didn't want to see or talk to anyone ever again.

Eleven

Todd dreaded going to school on Thursday morning, but he knew he had to face Mark. As he walked toward Sweet Valley Middle School, he realized he didn't even know if Mark would be there when he got to school. Maybe Mark had already been fired.

Todd kicked a stone into the street. He would tell Mr. Clark that it was all a mistake, that's what he'd do. But would Mr. Clark even listen?

At least no one was waiting for him at his locker, he thought when he reached the school. He went to homeroom. Patrick was standing outside the classroom talking to Sophia. "Hi," Todd said quietly.

Patrick and Sophia both looked at him, but neither of them said a word.

None of the kids in the writing class said anything when he took his seat in homeroom. Elizabeth wasn't there yet, but he guessed she had probably stopped talking to him too.

He put his head on his desk, wishing he was any place but school.

"I hear your father's trying to get the new writing teacher fired," Aaron said, leaning toward him. "Is that true?"

Todd lifted his head to look at Aaron. "I don't know what's happening," he said.

Aaron raised his eyebrows. "According to some of the kids in the class, you were trying to get yourself out of trouble for missing a basketball practice."

Todd felt his face turn red with anger. He had made a lot of mistakes lately, but blaming Mark wasn't one of them. "That's a lie," he said.

As soon as Mr. Davis entered the room, he turned and looked at Todd sternly. "Come here, Todd," he said.

Todd sighed. Great. Now he was in trouble with Mr. Davis, too.

"Mr. Clark wants to see you right away," Mr. Davis said when Todd had gotten to the front of the room.

"Mr. Clark?" Todd repeated in surprise.

"He told me you were to come to his office as soon as you got to school," Mr. Davis said. "So you'd better get going."

Todd nodded. He knew what Mr. Clark wanted. He was going to tell Todd that Mark had been fired.

*   *   *

Mr. Clark was sitting at his desk when Mrs. Knight, the office secretary, ushered Todd in.

"Sit down, Todd," Mr. Clark said after Mrs. Knight had closed the door. "I'm afraid I have some bad news," he said.

Here it comes, Todd thought. *He's going to tell me Mark's been fired.* Without even thinking, he opened his mouth and words started coming out. "Mr. Clark, I know it probably doesn't matter what I say, but Mark Ramirez is a great teacher. You shouldn't punish him for something I did."

Mr. Clark looked at him in surprise. "What's that?" he said. "Mark Ramirez?"

"Yes, Mr. Clark. He's a really good teacher. It's my fault he was fired."

"Fired!" Mr. Clark said. He rubbed his chin. "Is that why you think you're here? Because of Mr. Ramirez?"

Todd lowered his eyes. "Yes, sir," he said softly.

"I see," Mr. Clark said. He cleared his throat. "Todd, I appreciate your standing up for Mr. Ramirez like that, but that's not why you're here. Mr. Ramirez wasn't fired—"

Todd felt a surge of relief. Maybe there was still a chance for him to make everything right again. There was an important game tonight, he thought, his mind racing. Maybe if he helped the Gladiators win, it would make up for his losing the last game. Maybe he could show his father that Mark wasn't ruining his basketball game after all.

"I'm afraid it's more serious than that," Mr. Clark continued.

Todd's relief disappeared. More serious than almost getting a teacher fired?

Mr. Clark drummed his fingers on the desk. "Yesterday you left school without permission," he said. "That's a very serious offense at Sweet Valley Middle School."

Todd's eyes widened. How could he have been so stupid? He was so upset about Mark and the way everyone was treating him, he hadn't even thought about what would happen if he left school.

"Are you going to give me detention?" he asked, wondering how he would ever make it to basketball practice if he had to spend an hour after school every day for the next month. Or two.

Mr. Clark shook his head.

Good, Todd thought. It would ruin everything if he was late for the game tonight.

"Todd," Mr. Clark said, rising from his chair. "I'm afraid for an infraction this serious, the punishment must be serious too. Your punishment is suspension from the basketball team until further notice."

Todd felt the blood rush from his face. "But, Mr. Clark, there's a game today! I can't miss it!"

Mr. Clark went to the door and opened it in a gesture of dismissal. "I'm sorry, Todd," he said, "but I'm afraid you'll have to."

*   *   *

"Where's Todd?" Elizabeth asked Sophia, Amy, and Pamela just before English class. "I haven't seen him since yesterday."

Sophia shrugged. "Who cares? I saw him in homeroom this morning. He had to go to Mr. Clark's office."

"Mr. Clark's office!" Elizabeth exclaimed. "Why?"

Sophia shrugged again. "Beats me. Maybe he's mad because they didn't fire Mark."

Elizabeth frowned. "You're wrong, Sophia."

"How do you know?" Sophia asked.

Elizabeth sighed. "Because I had a talk with my mom last night and I put two and two together. We were unfair to Todd yesterday. I should know him better than that by this time. We all should. If Todd said it wasn't his idea to have Mark fired, I, for one, believe him." She shook her head. "Todd loves the writing class and he thinks Mark is a great teacher. This is Mr. Wilkins's idea." She gazed at the others. "Besides," she said, "it's when your friends are in trouble that you're supposed to stick by them."

Amy looked upset. "You're right, Elizabeth. We didn't even give him a chance to explain."

"I feel bad," Pamela said. "I was the one who started the whole thing."

Sophia nodded. "I wouldn't even say hi to him this morning."

"So where *is* he?" Amy asked.

"Maybe we should try to find him," Pamela suggested.

Amy's eyes widened. "Maybe he was suspended from school."

"He's not suspended from school," a voice from behind them said.

The girls turned around. It was Tim. "Todd's not suspended from school," Tim explained. "He's suspended from the basketball team." He shook his head. "Our final game before the championships, and no Todd. Just great, huh?"

Elizabeth felt terrible. If Todd had been suspended from the team, she knew he must be pretty upset. More than anything, she wanted to find him and make sure he was OK.

Tim shrugged. "I don't know where he is. The last I saw him, he was leaving school. I guess he figures he can't get into any more trouble than he's already in."

Elizabeth bit her lip. "Well, I guess there's nothing we can do right now. Maybe he needs some time to himself to think. But if he's not home by five o'clock, we'll start looking, OK?"

"That's when the game starts," Tim said. "He'll have to be home by then to tell his folks he's off the team." He shook his head. "That is, if he goes home at all."

"What do you mean?" Elizabeth demanded.

Tim shrugged. "It's just that if I was in as much trouble as Todd is in right now, I'd think twice about going home anytime soon. Mr. Wilkins is a real basketball fanatic. He won't be too thrilled when he hears that Todd's been kicked off the team."

Todd sat in his bedroom in the empty house, staring at the blank piece of paper in front of him on the desk. He had stayed at Secca Lake until two. His mother helped out at the homeless shelter on Thursday afternoons, and he knew she'd be gone by then.

He couldn't stop thinking about what a total disaster his life had become. He had no more friends, no more basketball, and no more writing. After walking out of school when he left Mr. Clark's office today, he probably wouldn't be allowed back into Sweet Valley Middle School at all.

He glanced at the clock radio beside his bed. It was almost four o'clock. His parents would probably both go straight to the basketball game without stopping at home first. What would they do when they found out he was suspended from the team? His father would be furious, Todd knew. He'd have Mark fired for sure this time.

Todd shook his head sadly. He felt terrible about Mark. He'd only been trying to help Todd make up his own mind. Todd also felt pretty bad about losing all his friends. No one had even tried to find him after he left school today. Not that he had wanted to be found—he had needed some time alone to think.

He sighed. Well, at least it made what he had to do easier—no one would miss him. He already knew there was only one way out of this.

He picked up his pen and started to write:

Dear Mom and Dad,
I'm sorry for disappointing you. I never meant to do it—it just happened. Please forgive me, but I just can't take it anymore. I've decided to run away. It's the only choice I have right now. I have enough money to get where I'm going. Please don't worry about me.
Love, Todd

He put the letter on top of his notebook, where his parents would be sure to find it. Then he went to his closet and pulled out the old coffee can he kept his money in. There was nearly fifty dollars in it. He'd been saving to buy a pair of pump basketball sneakers like Tim's.

He put the money in his pocket. *I guess I won't be needing those sneakers now,* he thought sadly. Then he took his duffel bag from the top shelf of his closet and stuffed a few changes of clothes into it.

He took his toothbrush and a comb from the bathroom, and put the picture of him and his parents that had sat on his bedside table for years on top of everything else in the duffel bag. Then he zipped the bag, closed his bedroom door, and steeled himself to say good-bye to Sweet Valley forever.

Twelve

"This is it," Jessica said. "This time we're buying some bras, no matter what." Jessica was sitting on Elizabeth's bed after school on Thursday, waiting for Elizabeth to get ready to go to the mall.

"Right," Elizabeth said, pulling on some black leggings and an oversize T-shirt. "You have to get to the basketball game, and I have to find Todd. We can't fool around this time."

Jessica nodded. "I already checked to make sure Mrs. Hunter wasn't working *and* that there were no ten-million-and-one sales." She frowned. "Aren't you ready yet?"

"Sorry," Elizabeth said. "I guess I'm a little distracted. I'm really kind of worried about Todd. We talked about him in Mark's class today."

"What did you decide?" Jessica asked, grabbing her sister's hairbrush.

"First, that we have to apologize for judging him guilty before we knew all the facts; and second, that we should always give our friends the benefit of the doubt."

"That sounds great," Jessica said. "But right now, I have to say that I *doubt* we'll get any bras unless we get moving."

Elizabeth glanced at her watch. "You're right, it's getting late."

As they left Elizabeth's room, Steven came bounding up the stairs. He looked at the twins' oversize T-shirts and grinned. "I know you two are growing up *and* out," he said, "but I think you're kidding yourselves if you think you'll ever be able to fill out *those* T-shirts."

"Ha, ha, Steven," Elizabeth said, rolling her eyes.

"Why don't you crawl back under your rock?" Jessica said.

"At least I might still *fit* under one," Steven said with a grin. He pulled out his shirt at chest level.

"What a jerk!" Elizabeth said, starting for the stairway.

"There are no Sweet Valley Middle School students here, did you notice?" Elizabeth said when she and Jessica walked into the mall.

"They're all getting ready to go to the basketball

game," Jessica said. "It's a big game. If we beat Johnson Middle School, we go to the district championships."

Elizabeth nodded, starting to worry about Todd again. "I know," she said, trying to push the thought out of her mind. "Let's get to Kendall's before some new disaster strikes."

The girls hurried past the perfume counter and the accessories department, and rode the escalator to the third floor. When they reached the lingerie department, they noticed the loud saleswoman. She was standing by the robes, hanging some new merchandise.

"Maybe she won't recognize us," Jessica said out of the corner of her mouth. But no sooner had she said it than the clerk came running over. "You're the *twins* who *ran* out of the *store* Saturday before *buying* your *bras*!" she shouted loudly enough for the next three departments to hear.

Elizabeth winced. "Yes," she said softly, hoping the woman would take the hint. "We, um, had an emergency."

The salesclerk shook her head. "What a *shame*!" she said as loudly as ever. "You missed a *great opportunity*! A woman came in right after you and ran off and bought *two Dreamline bras, just like yours*! Can you *imagine*? She's going to be in *all* our *ads* for an entire *year*!"

"Lucky her," Elizabeth whispered behind her hand.

Jessica giggled.

"So are we *back* to *buy* some *bras*?" the salesclerk asked.

"Yes, that's right," Elizabeth said quickly. "And we know exactly which ones we want." She grabbed Jessica by the hand and pulled her over to the Dreamline bras rack.

Jessica was shaking her head. "Maybe she needs a hearing aid or something."

"Or thinks *we* do," Elizabeth said.

"Let's just pay for these stupid bras and get out of here," Jessica muttered, grabbing two bras off the rack. "I really can't take another trip to Kendall's lingerie department."

"I'm with you," Elizabeth said.

The girls carried their bras over to the register. The saleswoman looked at the tags. "Oh," she exclaimed. "You girls are in luck! I think these *bras* are still on *sale!*"

Elizabeth and Jessica exchanged mortified glances. "Well, look at it this way," Elizabeth whispered. "We'll still have some money left over when we leave."

The salesclerk scratched her head. "Hmm, I was sure they were still on sale," she said a little more quietly, holding up the bras and gazing at them thoughtfully. "But the tags say full price." She shook her head. "Well," she said, grinning at the twins, "when in doubt, ask."

She cupped her hands around her mouth. "*Hey,*

Marge!" she screamed across the floor to the sales-woman by the dressing rooms. *"What's the sale price on these Dreamline training bras?"*

Elizabeth and Jessica ducked their heads, their faces beet-red.

"I think I'm going to die," Jessica moaned.

"Next time, let's buy our bras from a mail-order catalogue, all right?" Elizabeth whispered.

Finally the salesclerk rang up the bras, and Jessica and Elizabeth ran from the store, clutching the bags to their chests. "At last," Elizabeth gasped when they reached the parking lot. "Success!"

As the twins were walking home with their shopping bag, Elizabeth noticed clouds gathering in Sweet Valley's blue sky. "Oh, no!" she said. "It looks like it's going to rain again."

"We'd better hurry if we don't want to get soaked," Jessica said.

The twins began to walk faster. Suddenly some-one called from behind them, "Hey, Jessica and Elizabeth! Wait up!"

The girls stopped and turned around. Ken Matthews, Patrick Morris, and Aaron Dallas were coming down the street toward them. "What's up?" Ken asked when the boys drew closer.

Elizabeth pointed to the sky. "We're going to have a downpour any minute," she said.

Ken shrugged. "What's a little rain?"

Aaron opened his arms. "It doesn't bother me,"

he said. He looked at Jessica. "Hey, Jessica, aren't you supposed to be with the Boosters at the basketball game today?"

Jessica nodded. "We had to buy something first."

"What?" Aaron asked.

Jessica looked at Elizabeth, horrified. "Um, just some, um . . ."

"Sweat socks!" Elizabeth finished for her. "Jessica needed some new sweat socks for the game tonight."

"Oh," Aaron said, looking a little puzzled. "Well, I guess if you need sweat socks, you need sweat socks." He glanced at his watch. "Wow!" he said. "You'd better hurry if you're going to get to the game in time, Jessica. It's already four o'clock."

"Four o'clock!" Jessica exclaimed. She grabbed Elizabeth's arm. "Let's go, Lizzie!"

"Hold on a minute!" Ken said before the girls could run off. The clouds grew darker. A clap of thunder sounded in the distance.

Jessica and Elizabeth stopped and turned around.

"Have either of you seen Todd? We were trying to find him before the game. Mark Ramirez talked to Mr. Clark and convinced him to change his mind about Todd's punishment. He explained about Todd's father and all that stuff, you know. Anyway, Mr. Clark said Todd could play in the game tonight. He'll just have to hang out in detention for a few weeks instead—" He grinned.

"—but only on non–basketball days, of course."

Elizabeth felt her heart soar. "Really? That's great!" she exclaimed. "Todd will be so happy! We've got to find him! Did you try his house?"

"We called there first," Aaron said. "No one answered."

"Oh," Elizabeth said, disappointed. Thunder boomed overhead, making the girls jump.

"Wow!" Jessica said. "We'd better get going!"

But before they could move, huge drops of rain began falling all around them. Suddenly the sky opened up in a cloudburst.

The five of them ran across the street toward the shelter of a dry cleaner's awning. They were sopping wet by the time they crowded beneath it.

"A lot of good *that* did," Jessica said a few minutes later when the downpour stopped. She twisted the water out of her T-shirt.

"Look at it this way, Jess," Elizabeth said. "You won't need to shower before the game."

Jessica turned to the boys. "We've really got to get going," she said, trying to look as unflustered as possible under the circumstances. "I'm going to be late."

"See you!" the boys called as the twins started to walk away.

"Call me if you find Todd," Elizabeth called over her shoulder. "I'm going to start looking for him too."

"No problem," Aaron called.

The girls had gone about twelve feet when they

heard Aaron shouting again. "Hey, Jessica! I think you dropped something!"

Jessica looked down at her rain-soaked Kendall's bag and gasped. Her heart dropped down to her toes. "Oh no!" she cried.

"What's the matter?" Elizabeth asked. Suddenly her eyes fell on the shopping bag. "Oh no!" she echoed.

The two girls stared in shock at the patch of sidewalk through the hole in the bottom of the wet bag.

They turned around, their faces filled with horror. Lying on the sidewalk behind them, in full view of the three boys, were two brand-new Dreamline bras.

Thirteen

It was getting dark by the time Todd left his house. The phone had rung about an hour earlier, but he hadn't answered it. He had thought it might be one of his parents. They would understand why he hadn't answered when they found the note.

The neighborhood was very quiet. He figured almost everyone must be at the game. He thought how it would feel to be on the court right now, playing against Johnson Middle School with the championship slot at stake. He'd be really nervous. But he'd also be excited, adrenaline pumping through his veins. He wondered if the Gladiators would win or lose, and if they won, who would make the winning shot.

But he shouldn't think about things like that now, he reminded himself. He was off the team.

Soon he would be leaving that, and everything else about Sweet Valley Middle School, behind him for good.

He took one last look at his house, then started down the sidewalk, his eyes on the ground.

As he walked down the street toward the bus station, he heard someone calling his name.

He turned around, surprised, and saw Elizabeth running toward him.

"Todd! Wait up!" She pounded down the sidewalk toward him. "I'm really sorry for what I said yesterday afternoon," Elizabeth said breathlessly when she reached him. "I know it wasn't you who tried to get Mark fired. I had just found out about it when I saw you, and I guess I was upset."

Todd shrugged. It didn't matter anymore. "That's OK," he said.

Elizabeth glanced at his duffel bag. "Where are you going?"

"I, uh, just cleaned out my closet," he lied. "I'm taking some clothes to the homeless shelter before they close." He was afraid that if he told Elizabeth what he was really doing, she'd tell his parents.

"I'll walk to the shelter with you," Elizabeth offered.

"No!" Todd snapped.

Elizabeth looked startled.

"I mean, I'm really in a hurry," Todd said.

Elizabeth looked down at her feet. "Todd, I don't blame you for being angry with me. I was wrong not to trust you. Everyone was wrong, except for Mark. Mark never thought you were trying to get him fired for a second." At the mention of Mark, Elizabeth suddenly remembered about the basketball game and Mr. Clark.

"Oh, no!" she said. "I almost forgot! Mr. Clark said—"

"Listen, Elizabeth, I've really got to go," Todd said, walking away.

"But Mr. Clark said you could play in tonight's game!" Elizabeth glanced at her watch. "If you hurry, you can still make it for the second half."

Todd stopped. He stared at her for a moment. This morning he would have been thrilled at the news. But it was too late. He'd already made his decision to leave Sweet Valley. "I've given up basketball," he said.

"But, Todd—" Elizabeth began.

"Elizabeth, I'm sorry," Todd said, "but I have to get these clothes to the homeless shelter before they close."

Elizabeth looked at the duffel bag. "If that's what you really want to do," she said.

"It's what I *have* to do," Todd said.

Elizabeth watched Todd walk away. Something was very wrong. She had volunteered at the homeless shelter for a while and she knew the office closed at five on Thursdays. Elizabeth felt certain that something strange was up.

She waited until Todd turned the corner, then she

began to follow him, keeping close to the shadows of trees and bushes. It was something she'd learned from the Amanda Howard novels she'd read.

She followed Todd up to Yale Avenue, past Some Crumb Bakery. It was really getting dark now. *Where is he going?* Elizabeth wondered. He was heading toward the canning factory, not the homeless shelter. The factory was in the most run-down section of town. There was nothing else around there except a lot of abandoned warehouses.

Her hand flew to her mouth. *And the Sweet Valley bus station!*

She followed Todd for two more blocks, until she was certain that that was where he was headed. Then she turned around and ran as fast as she could to the Sweet Valley Middle School gym. If someone didn't stop Todd soon, they might never see him again!

She crossed her fingers. *Wherever you're planning on going, Todd,* she thought, *I sure hope your bus isn't waiting at the station!*

Todd glanced behind him. He didn't see anyone around, but he had the creepy feeling he was being followed. He clutched his duffel bag tighter and started walking faster. Dark shadows followed him across Yale Avenue toward the canning factory and the Sweet Valley bus station.

He patted his back pocket to make sure his money was still there. He planned to go to San

Diego and stay with Anthony, his best friend from camp. *How much does a ticket to San Diego cost?* he wondered. He hoped fifty dollars was enough.

The bus station was eerily quiet when he stepped inside. Except for the ticket seller and an old man in tattered clothes sleeping on one of the orange benches that lined the wall, Todd was alone.

He put his duffel bag down on one of the orange seats in the middle of the station and went to the ticket counter. "One way to San Diego, please," he said.

The ticket seller nodded and pushed his glasses up on his nose. "That'll be twenty-five fifty," he said. Todd gulped. He hadn't realized it would be so much. Once he got to San Diego he would have to find a job. Maybe he could sell newspapers or mow people's lawns.

He handed the ticket seller thirty dollars and waited for his change. When he'd gotten his ticket he sat down on the chair beside his duffel bag. Suddenly he felt very tired.

He stuffed his ticket into his back pocket with the rest of his money, where it would be safe. According to the schedule above the ticket seller's window, the bus to San Diego wasn't leaving for another hour. What was he going to do for an hour? There were five-inch-screen televisions attached to the orange chairs, but they cost twenty-five cents for every five minutes. He'd go broke feeding quarters into one of them for an hour.

He glanced around the station. Maybe someone had left a newspaper or a magazine or something to read. Finally his eyes settled on the second hand on the clock above the schedule. He watched it for a while as it made its way around the clock again and again and again. His eyelids grew heavy. Soon he was sound asleep.

"Todd?" a voice said gently.

Todd's eyelids fluttered open. For a moment he'd forgotten where he was.

"Todd?"

The bus station. He was at the bus station waiting for a bus to San Diego. He turned to the voice beside him.

It was his dad, sitting in the orange plastic seat next to his.

"How did you find me?" Todd asked.

"Elizabeth Wakefield ran to the gym and told me where you were going," his father said.

"But how did she know?" Todd asked.

His father sighed. "She was worried about you," he said. "She followed you to the bus station."

Todd stared at his hands. "I thought someone was following me," he said. "I should have known it was Elizabeth."

He and his father sat in silence after that, for what seemed like a very long time. Mr. Wilkins nervously cracked his knuckles.

"I missed you at the game today," he said finally.

"Everyone did. The team won, but just barely. Coach Cassels said they all want you back."

Todd shrugged. "I'm not sure I can go back," he said.

His father nodded. "Yes, you can. I talked to Mr. Clark. I explained why you left school." He paused. "I talked to Mark Ramirez today too."

"You did?" Todd asked without looking at his father.

His father let out a long breath. "Yes, I did. I wish I'd talked to him sooner. He's a pretty nice guy."

Todd looked at his father in surprise. He felt his heart thudding in his chest.

Mr. Wilkins nodded slowly. "Mark said you're a very talented writer. He also thinks you're quite a basketball player. He thinks you should do what you want to do."

Todd shook his head wearily. "That's what I was trying to tell you. I can't. I can't make a choice about what I want to do until I find out what that is. And the only way I can find that out is by trying different things."

His father nodded again. "I understand that now. You have to make your own decisions." He cleared his throat. "But just so you know, son—you're much more important to me than basketball ever was."

Todd met his father's eyes. He could see a sadness and gentleness there that he had never seen before. For a moment Todd felt overwhelmed with a sense of relief. "I know, Dad," he said, trying to keep his voice even.

His father put his arm around Todd's shoulders. "I heard you wrote a great story," he said. He cleared his throat again. "Do you think I could read it one of these days?"

Todd smiled. He felt his eyes fill with tears. He waited until he could get the words out without his voice breaking. "I'd love that, Dad. I thought you'd never ask."

". . . so I bought a ticket to San Diego," Todd told the group of his friends who were listening to his story at the lunch table the next day, "but luckily my dad found me in time." He smiled at Elizabeth. "With a little help from Elizabeth."

"Wow!" Aaron said. "The farthest I've ever run away is Secca Lake. But I was only a kid at the time."

Patrick grinned. "When was that, Aaron, last year?"

Everyone laughed.

Maria shook her head in amazement. "That would make a great story for Mark's class, you know?" she said. Then she raised one eyebrow quizzically. "If you plan to *stay* in Mark's class, that is."

Todd smiled. "I do. I might even become a writer someday."

Elizabeth glanced at Maria, then at Todd. "But what about basketball?" she asked.

Todd sat back in his chair, his hands behind his head. "I'm going to do that, too," he said. "Coach Cassels, Mark, and I had a talk this morning. The coach is going to let me start practice ten minutes later so I can make it to the gym on time. And Mark's going to keep our homework down to a few hours a week. That is, if it's OK with the rest of the class."

"Oh, no!" Patrick said. "Not less homework!" He pretended to keel over and faint.

Just then Maria nudged Elizabeth. "Look over there," she said.

Elizabeth looked over at the Unicorner, where Jessica, Lila, and Ellen were sitting. They were all fanning themselves with pieces of folded paper and batting their eyelashes at every boy who walked by.

"I know the Unicorns are flirts," Maria said, "but that's ridiculous. What's going on?"

"Beats me," Elizabeth said.

"I think I know," Pamela said, reaching into her notebook. "The teacher passed this out in social studies today." She handed Elizabeth a sheet of paper.

"It's a list of books about the Old South," Elizabeth said, scanning it. She looked up, confused. "What does this have to do with the Unicorns?"

"We're going to be learning about slavery and the great plantations, and the cotton trade, and even voodoo," Pamela explained, shrugging. "I guess the Unicorns are just getting into the whole Old South mentality."

"Did you say voodoo?" Maria asked. She glanced over at Jessica and Lila, who were talking to each other behind their fans. "Well, at least right now they seem more interested in the Southern-belles part than in voodoo," she said.

Elizabeth nodded. "Yeah, it was bad enough when Jessica thought she had extrasensory powers. The last thing I need is for her to start fooling around with voodoo."

Maria nodded. "My grandmother had a friend who knew about voodoo. She says it's nothing to play with."

What will happen when Jessica starts experimenting with voodoo? Find out in Sweet Valley Twins and Friends #78, **STEVEN THE ZOMBIE.**

SIGN UP FOR THE SWEET VALLEY HIGH® FAN CLUB!

Hey, girls! Get all the gossip on Sweet
Valley High's® most popular teenagers
when you join our fantastic Fan Club!
As a member, you'll get all of this really
cool stuff:

- Membership Card with your own
  personal Fan Club ID number
- A Sweet Valley High® Secret
  Treasure Box
- Sweet Valley High® Stationery
- Official Fan Club Pencil (for secret
  note writing!)
- Three Bookmarks
- A "Members Only" Door Hanger
- Two Skeins of J. & P. Coats® Embroidery
  Floss with flower barrette instruction
  leaflet
- Two editions of *The Oracle* newsletter
- Plus exclusive Sweet Valley High®
  product offers, special savings,
  contests, and much more!

Be the first to find out what Jessica & Elizabeth Wakefield are up to by joining the
Sweet Valley High® Fan Club for the one-year membership fee of only $6.25 each
for U.S. residents, $8.25 for Canadian residents (U.S. currency). Includes shipping
& handling.

Send a check or money order (do not send cash) made payable to "Sweet Valley
High® Fan Club" along with this form to:

SWEET VALLEY HIGH® FAN CLUB, BOX 3919-B, SCHAUMBURG, IL 60168-3919

NAME_____
                              (Please print clearly)

ADDRESS_____

CITY_____ STATE _____ ZIP_____
                                                              (Required)

AGE _____ BIRTHDAY_____ /_____ /_____

Offer good while supplies last. Allow 6-8 weeks after check clearance for delivery. Addresses without ZIP
codes cannot be honored. Offer good in USA & Canada only. Void where prohibited by law.
©1993 by Francine Pascal   LCI-1383-193

THE UNICORN CLUB

HANG WITH THE COOLEST KIDS AROUND!

Jessica and Elizabeth Wakefield are just two of the terrific members of The Unicorn Club you've met in *Sweet Valley Twins and Friends*. Now get to know some of their friends even better! Share in their exciting adventures with this great new series. Join The Unicorn Club and become a part of the friendship and fun!

A Sensational NEW Sweet Valley Series!

NOW READ THE BOOK!

Based on the Warner Bros. motion picture and Emmy award-winning television show.

BATMAN'S PAST COMES BACK TO HAUNT HIM

A friend from long ago returns to Gotham City—someone who knows secrets about Batman even his mysterious identity can't hide. Find out if Batman will be able to put aside his feelings about this surprise arrival as he battles a menacing band of mobsters and a terrifying new enemy.

❑ BATMAN: Mask of the Phantasm—The Animated Movie
Novelization by Andrew Helfer
Based on an original screenplay by Alan Burnett
0-553-48174-6 $3.99/$4.99 Can.
